How to Catch a Cowboy

How to Catch a Cowboy

A Riverrun Ranch Romance

Karen Foley

TULE
PUBLISHING

Chapter One

S HE SPOTTED HIM as soon as he walked through the door of Rosa's Cantina: six-and-a-half feet of deliciously muscled, wide-shouldered, lean-hipped magnificence. He was a hard man to miss and more than one woman's gaze locked on to him as he strode into the restaurant. He took off his Stetson and dragged a hand through the thick, brown layers of his hair as he scanned the interior. Jessie Montero's pulse quickened when his blue eyes found her, lingered for a heartbeat, and then moved on.

Jessie had known Holt Claiborne her entire life and had harbored a crush on him for half of it. She only wished he could see her as a desirable woman and not just the girl who served up his favorite carne asada every Thursday night at Rosa's Cantina, the Mexican restaurant she helped her father run on the outskirts of Last Stand, Texas. Her grandfather had purchased the restaurant just weeks before he married Jessie's grandmother, Rosa-Maria, and had named the cantina after his bride. More than forty years had passed since then. But there had always been a cantina on this site, even before the skirmish that occurred during the Texas Revolution, when a group of local men had holed themselves up in the saloon and successfully held off a band of Mexican soldiers. The small, brief battle gave the town of Last Stand both an identity and a name. A marker located in town provided the names of the heroes involved, including Sherman "Shotgun" Claiborne, Holt's great-great-grandfather. Rumor had it that he had abducted the beautiful daughter of a local Mexican rancher and forced her at gunpoint to marry him. Nobody knew for certain if that part of the story was true, but the marriage had apparently been a happy one, producing a half dozen children.

Looking at Holt now, Jessie thought he wouldn't need to force her to marry him. All he'd need to do is ask and she'd run off with him. Not that that was likely to happen. Holt had been married once, years ago. It had ended badly and some said he'd sworn never to get married again. Not that Jessie was looking for a husband, but she wouldn't say no to a little romance. Or even better, a torrid love affair. Although that wasn't likely, either, she thought dismally. She'd been friends with Holt's two younger sisters since childhood, and her grandmother, Rosa-Maria, had been the Claibornes' housekeeper and cook at Riverrun Ranch for more than twenty years. If Holt thought of her at all, it was probably as a family friend and nothing more.

She needed to change that.

Tonight, he was with his two younger brothers, Evan and Luke. They were twins, but not identical. Technically, they were Holt's half brothers. Their father, Gus Claiborne, had been married three times and had children from each marriage, and a fifth child from an affair he'd had during his last marriage. Now the three men sat down at a table near the bar.

"I'll take this one," Jessie said to Katie, one of the waitresses.

"But you're not even a server," Katie protested. "You're the manager. You shouldn't be waiting tables."

"These guys are . . . special," she said. Katie was new to the restaurant, so she didn't yet realize that Jessie waited on the Claiborne brothers whenever they came into Rosa's Cantina. "My grandmother works for them and we've known the family forever. Call it a professional courtesy."

She loaded a basket filled with warm tortilla chips and a bowl of homemade salsa onto a tray and made her way through the restaurant to their table. The cantina was crowded and noisy, the Mexican guitar music that played through unseen speakers competing with the sounds of people talking and laughing. Overhead, dozens of brightly colored bulbs gave the large room a festive atmosphere, and strings of papel picado banners, cut from colorful tissue paper, crisscrossed the antique-tin ceiling.

"Good evening, boys," Jessie said cheerfully as she set the food down on the table. She couldn't help sliding a hopeful glance at Holt, but he was focused on his menu with a single-minded intensity, as if he'd never seen it before and had no idea what to order. That might have worked, if he hadn't been coming to the cantina every Thursday night for the past eight years.

He was deliberately trying to avoid talking to her.

"Hey, Jessie," Luke said with a friendly smile.

"Nice to see you, Jess," Evan added, giving her a cheeky wink. "As always."

Unlike his brothers, Holt didn't greet her. The only indication he was even aware of her was a small crease that appeared between his dark eyebrows. Not quite a frown, Jessie thought, but pretty darn close.

"What's wrong, Holt?" she asked. "Cat got your tongue, as well as your manners?"

He did look up then, ignoring Evan's amused snicker. The pure blueness of his eyes always made Jessie feel a little dazzled, but when his gaze locked on to hers, she actually felt the floor tilt beneath her feet.

"There's absolutely nothing wrong with my tongue," he drawled.

His words caused all kinds of juicy images to swirl through her vivid imagination as she struggled to form a response. "So, it's just the manners, then."

"I'm still working on those."

Evan made a small scoffing noise and said something that sounded like, *Yeah, right*.

"Ah," Jessie murmured. "Maybe you need an experienced handler."

For just an instant, something flared in his eyes, like the blue flame of a gas burner. Then it was gone and Jessie wondered if she had only imagined that incandescent flash of heat.

After a scant second, when it became obvious he wasn't going to respond to her provocative statement, Jessie drew in a deep breath and turned her attention back to the twins, who were as different in temperament as they were in looks. "The usual for both of you?"

"You know us too well," Luke said with a warm smile. "The usual, and a round of beer for the table."

The usual consisted of the house special or *Tres Compadres*, a plate consisting of premium grilled skirt steak, grilled chicken, and a marinated shrimp skewer with all the sides. Holt was still studying the menu, but Jessie knew he would order the carne asada, as he always did.

"You got it," Jessie said.

She liked Luke, whose girlfriend, Jorie, had been her best friend since middle school. Luke had recently returned to Last Stand after a twelve-year stint in the army as a K9 handler. Both he and his service dog had been injured in combat, but Luke had been able to adopt Elsa, his devoted German shepherd, and the two were nearly inseparable.

Luke and Jorie were building a house together out on Hickory Creek Road and Jessie couldn't be happier for them. With his military law enforcement background, Luke could come across as tough and insensitive, but Jessie knew he had a heart of pure gold and would do anything for those he loved. And he loved Jorie Russell, the lucky girl.

Jessie wanted what her friend had. Not with Luke, of course, but with Holt.

She liked Evan, too, but he rarely took life seriously, and could usually be seen with a different girl every weekend at the Last Stand Saloon. When he wasn't working cattle, he volunteered as a firefighter for the Last Stand Fire Department.

She was swinging away from the table when Holt's voice stopped her. "Tequila."

She turned. "Excuse me?"

Holt leaned back in his chair and his eyes glinted with lazy humor. "I'd like a tequila, please. Neat."

Jessie felt the impact of that volatile blue gaze all the way to her toes, which were curling inside her Tony Lama boots.

"Any particular brand?" The cantina had an impressive collection of tequilas, ranging from five-dollar shots to some that would set a customer back more than two hundred bucks. Holt didn't always order tequila but when he did, he usually chose a ten- or twelve-dollar shot.

"Surprise me," he said, and turned his attention back to the menu.

His tone said he didn't particularly care what brand she selected. He hadn't been rude, exactly, just . . . indifferent. To both the tequila and to her.

She'd had a thing for him for as long as she could remember, but no matter what she did to try to gain the handsome rancher's attention, he seemed determined to ignore her. From the time she'd turned eighteen and had begun working at the cantina, she'd been asked out by more cowboys than she could keep track of, so it wasn't as if she was ugly. In fact, she'd been called gorgeous.

Sultry.

Her looks aside, she was smart, hardworking, loyal, and passionate. Any guy would be lucky to have her. Call her crazy, but she was only interested in one guy, who apparently neither knew nor cared about her existence. The thought filled her first with sadness and then with a kind of fierce determination.

"You got it," she said sweetly and spun on her heel, flipping her ponytail over her shoulder. How many times had her mother warned her that one day her impetuous nature would get her into trouble? Right now, she didn't care. She would get a reaction out of Holt Claiborne if it was the last thing she did.

She signaled to Ruis, the bartender.

"Three Bud Lights and . . ." She paused, perusing the selection of tequila on the top shelf behind the bar. "A shot of 1800 Coleccion."

Ruis's eyebrows shot up and he gave a low whistle. "Who's the big spender?"

Jessie shrugged as she placed the three bottles of Bud Light on the tray and watched as Ruis drew down a full-bellied snifter glass and carefully measured out the golden liquor. "Holt Claiborne."

Ruis shot her a startled look. "Seriously? He almost never orders tequila and, when he does, it's always Patron."

Jessie took the snifter and placed it on the tray next to the beers. "I asked him if he had a preference, and he told me to surprise him. So this is me, surprising him."

Ruis had worked at the cantina for more than ten years, and Jessie looked on him more as a big brother than a coworker or employee. She trusted him, and had always appreciated that he treated her as a friend and not an employer.

"At one-hundred-thirty bucks a pop?" Ruis shook his

head. "Not cool, Jess."

Ignoring him, Jessie picked up the tray and brought it over to the table. "Here you go," she said and placed the drinks on the table, sliding the snifter toward Holt. "Ready to order?"

She watched as Holt raised the glass and swirled the amber liquid, before lifting it to his nose and inhaling. If he suspected he'd been served a luxury tequila, he gave no indication. But she noted how he didn't throw the tequila back in one swallow. Instead, he sipped it, and his blue eyes closed for a moment as he savored the drink. Jessie couldn't help but stare at him, riveted by the look of sublime pleasure on his face. Only the sound of Luke clearing his throat in a meaningful way drew her back to her surroundings.

"Do you know what you'd like to eat?"

Holt set the snifter down and looked at her, and in that instant, Jessie knew that he knew what she had done. The faintest hint of a smile lurked in one corner of his mouth and his eyes gleamed. "If I didn't already have my heart set on the carne asada, I'd tell you to surprise me."

Jessie's heart skipped erratically beneath that shrewd look, but she forced herself to give him a placid smile. "Carne asada it is."

As she walked back toward the kitchen, she couldn't help glancing over her shoulder at Holt. Leaning forward, he said something to his brothers as he swirled his tequila, causing them to laugh, and then all three of them looked directly at her. Holt lifted his glass and Jessie's face burned as she quickly ducked into the kitchen to place their order. She would pay for the tequila, of course. She didn't know what had possessed her to bring him one of the most expensive liquors they carried, but there was no doubt she had achieved her goal.

Holt had definitely noticed her.

Amanda, one of the serving staff at the restaurant, and a good friend of Jessie's, sidled up to her. "So? What's going on? I saw him talking to you."

Jessie tucked a loose strand of hair behind one ear. "That wasn't talking. He just ordered his usual carne asada. No big deal."

"Well, he must be in a good mood if he ordered the top-shelf tequila. What's he celebrating?"

"He's not." Jessie slanted her a rueful grin. "He wanted tequila and he told me to surprise him."

Amanda's eyes widened and she gave a choked bark of laughter. "So you ordered him a hundred-and-something-dollar shot?"

Jessie rounded her eyes in mock innocence. "Was that bad of me?"

"Ha. I hope you're not expecting a tip," Amanda said with a grin.

When Jessie carried their meals to the table, she half expected Holt to call her out on the hoax, but he didn't.

"Would you like another round of drinks?" she asked as she set the dishes down. "Maybe another tequila?"

Holt's eyes held a knowing glint. "No, thanks. Another round of beers should do it."

Jessie held his gaze for a second longer than necessary,

then slowly picked up the empty bottles before turning on her heel and walking toward the bar. This time, she didn't look back. She set the empties down on the bar top and swiped a hand across her eyes. She didn't know why she bothered.

Short of stripping naked and dancing on his table, she doubted he would ever see her as a desirable woman. Jorie had once claimed Holt was the most intimidating of the three Claiborne brothers and that she'd be terrified to even flirt with him. But Jessie suspected his aloof manner was a deliberate ruse to keep women—*all women*—away. At least, any women who might look at him as a potential husband. And who could blame him? His own mother died when he was an infant and, as a boy, he'd watched two stepmothers walk out on the family. He'd shocked everyone when he'd decided to get married right out of college, but he'd soon discovered his young wife had been cheating on him. Adding insult to injury, she'd dragged Holt through a long, ugly divorce and from what Jessie had heard, his ex had taken him to the cleaners.

It was for precisely that reason Jessie stopped short of making any kind of overt pass at him. She knew instinctively he wouldn't respond to that kind of advance and might even find it offensive. Surprisingly, his conservative nature was one of the things she liked best about Holt Claiborne. Her favorite fantasy involved her making him lose control. But how to do that when he seemed determined to ignore her? She could swish her hips and show off her cleavage with the best, but not in her family's restaurant. She'd considered spending more time at Riverrun Ranch on the pretext of visiting her grandmother, but even that seemed just shy of stalking him.

Blowing out a hard breath, Jessie loaded another round of beers onto her tray. As she carried them back toward the table, she became aware of two things: Holt was speaking into his cell phone even as his eyes followed her progress with a strange intensity, and her father, Jose Montero, strode out of the kitchen wearing a distressed expression that caused alarm bells to jangle in her head. She reached the Claiborne table at the same time her father did and the two men exchanged a meaningful look. Before Jessie had a chance to set the tray down, Holt was removing it from her hands.

"What?" She locked her gaze on to her father's anguished face. "What's happened?"

"It's Rosa-Maria," Holt said, pulling out his wallet and dropping two crisp hundred-dollar bills onto the table. "She's had a heart attack."

Chapter Two

H OLT'S FATHER WAS at the hospital when they arrived. He sat in a chair in the waiting area with his face buried in his hands and he looked so lost, Holt's heart hitched in alarm. In his midsixties, Gus Claiborne was a man who commanded respect and rarely lost control of his emotions. Seeing him like this unnerved Holt.

"Dad?"

Gus raised his head and, for a moment, his expression was desolate. Then, seeing Holt and the twins, he stood up and managed a reassuring smile. But Holt wasn't fooled. His father was scared.

"She's going to be okay," Gus said quickly. "They're running some tests now." He looked past Holt to the sliding glass doors that led to the parking lot. "Where are Jose and Jessie? I thought they would come with you."

Holt had offered to drive them himself, but Jose had insisted on taking his own vehicle, probably knowing he wouldn't leave the hospital that night.

"They're right behind us," Holt assured him.

Even as he said the words, the glass doors slid open again and Jessie and her father hurried inside. Jessie had been crying; Holt could see the tear tracks on her cheeks and there was a sheen of moisture in her beautiful brown eyes. Her lower lip trembled, as if she was barely holding it together. Something twisted in his chest. In all the years he'd known Jessie, he'd never seen her cry. His brothers would be surprised to know he'd even noticed, but he had. There wasn't much about Jessica Montero that escaped his notice, like the fact she was hands down the most beautiful woman he'd ever set eyes on.

He still remembered the first time he'd noticed her as a woman and not as Rosa-Maria's granddaughter or his kid sister's friend. It was five years ago, and he and Evan had been kicking back at the Last Stand Saloon when a group of young women came in, laughing and lighting the place up with their boisterous energy. But when one of the women had begun dancing to the music, uncaring that she had no partner, Holt had been unable to stop staring. Wearing a breezy little dress and flat sandals, with her dark hair falling around her shoulders, she was incandescent. Before long, every guy in the place was watching her solo performance, while her girlfriends hooted and clapped and encouraged her.

"Well, damn," Evan had said, setting his beer down. "She's definitely had a few too many. I'd better take her home or these cowpokes will be on her faster than a duck on a June bug."

He'd stood, but Holt had forestalled him with a hand on his arm. "You know her?"

Evan's expression had been almost comical. "Holt, that's Jessie! Rosa-Maria's granddaughter. Callie and Emmaline's friend? You don't recognize her?"

Holt had been stunned. When had Jessica Montero grown up? And how had he not noticed?

"Christ," he'd muttered. "Is she actually old enough to drink?"

"I think she's celebrating her twenty-first birthday tonight," Evan had replied. "Uh-oh, here comes Billy Gonzalez. I'd better get her home before he does something that makes me have to punch him."

In the end, Holt had gone with his brother and together, they'd accompanied the entire birthday group back to Jessie's house, where her parents had thanked them and ushered the rowdy young women into the house.

But it was too late for him to simply do a good deed and then forget about her; Holt was smitten.

Now Jessie clung to her father, but it was unclear who was supporting whom. Seeing Gus, she managed a smile and hurried forward to hug the older man.

"Thank you so much for getting her here so fast," she said. "I still can't believe it. She's always been so healthy!"

"When can we see her?" Jose had rushed out of the restaurant so fast, he hadn't even removed his chef's apron. In his midforties, he was a handsome man with curly black hair and expressive dark eyes.

"They're running tests now," Gus said. "The doctor said he'd let us know as soon as she's able to have visitors."

"But what happened?" Jessie asked.

Gus rubbed a hand across the back of his neck, his blue eyes clouded. "She has Thursday nights off, as you know.

Even though I've told her it's not necessary, she always leaves me dinner on the kitchen island; just a sandwich or a bowl of soup, nothing big." He paused. "I went into the kitchen and was surprised to see her there. I thought she had gone out for the night. She was tidying the kitchen and we were talking, and then suddenly she just—"

He broke off.

"It's okay, Dad," Luke said. "She's in good hands now, and she's going to be fine."

"The doctor told me you did everything right, giving her an aspirin and calling for an ambulance," Jose said. "Thank you for that."

"Here comes the doc now," Holt observed.

They turned to see Dr. Rick Wallace walking toward them. In his early thirties and good-looking, he was popular with the ladies, but he also had a reputation as an excellent ER doctor. He smiled reassuringly as they crowded around him.

"Mrs. Montero had a mild heart attack," he said. "Her potassium and sugar levels are also high, so we're going to keep her here for a few days until we get both under control."

"But she's going to be fine." Gus said it as a statement, as if it was a foregone conclusion.

"Yes, I believe she will make a full recovery," Dr. Wallace said. "There doesn't appear to be any damage to the heart muscle, but we'll consult with our cardiologist, Dr. Fletcher, just to be certain. Mrs. Montero will need to take it easy for a time."

"Thank God," Gus muttered.

Holt sharpened his attention on his father. Rosa-Maria had worked in the Claiborne home for nearly twenty-five years, so his worry was natural, but Holt saw something more in his father's reaction, something other than just an employer's concern for an employee. The older man had actually buckled a bit when the doctor had assured them Rosa-Maria would be okay.

"Can we see her?" Jessie asked.

"Of course. She's resting comfortably, but I don't want to overtax her, so . . ." Dr. Wallace assessed the small group. "Gus, Jose, and Jessie, you can go in now. Guys, you can see her tomorrow, after she's had some rest."

Holt nodded. "Of course. I'll wait for you, Dad, if that's okay."

Gus paused. "Sure you don't want to head home, son? There's nothing you can do here tonight."

"Rosa-Maria is family." Holt gestured toward his brothers. "I don't think any of us want to leave until we hear from you on her condition."

Gus nodded. "Okay, son. We won't be long."

Jessie looked at him then, her dark gaze clinging to his as her father led her past him and down the corridor. When they turned a corner and disappeared from sight, Holt blew out a hard breath and scrubbed a hand across the back of his neck.

"You heard the doc," Evan said, watching him. "She's going to be okay."

"Yeah," Holt muttered. "Thank Christ."

Evan gave him a crooked grin. "My thoughts, exactly. Because your cooking skills are shit, and mine aren't much better."

"Jesus, that's cold, Evan." This came from Luke, who until now had stood to one side, observing. "I can cook your damned breakfast, if that's the issue."

"Nobody wants you to do the cooking." Holt gave his brother a tolerant look. "You've got your own life. We'll figure something out until Rosa-Maria is back on her feet, but I don't think we need to hire anyone to fill in until then. We're grown-ass men and we can damn well cook and clean up after ourselves."

He didn't miss the look that passed between the twins. Clearly, they had their doubts.

"That was a joke about the cooking, by the way." Evan removed his cowboy hat and pushed his fingers through his hair. "I just want her to be okay too."

"Yeah, we all do." Holt sat down in the chair his father had vacated.

He hadn't exaggerated when he'd said Rosa-Maria was family. She'd been the single stabilizing female presence in their lives when their own mothers hadn't been there.

"Do Emmaline and Callie know?"

Neither of their younger half sisters had been raised at Riverrun Ranch, but both had spent a great deal of time there during their childhood. During their visits, Rosa-Maria had taken them under her wing as if they had been her own daughters. They would want to know what had happened.

"I'll give them both a call now," Evan said.

Holt couldn't imagine Riverrun Ranch without Rosa-Maria there. But Evan made a good point; if she needed time to recover, they'd have to divvy up the household tasks, at least temporarily. Maybe the meals wouldn't be as good as Rosa-Maria's, but they'd get by.

❧

"YOU WANT ME to take over as the cook at Riverrun Ranch?" Jessie asked in astonishment.

Her grandmother lay in the hospital bed, gripping Jessie's hands in her own. She had an oxygen tube in her nose and her complexion looked waxy, but her dark eyes were bright with determination. Beside her, a heart monitor emitted reassuring, rhythmic beeps.

"Yes. It's the perfect solution."

Jessie glanced toward the door. Rosa-Maria had ordered both Gus and Jose out of the room, insisting she needed to speak privately with Jessie. Now the two men were pacing impatiently in the hallway, no doubt curious as to what Rosa-Maria needed to talk with her about.

"*Abuela*, you're not thinking clearly," Jessie said gently. "I already have a job at the cantina. Why would I agree to cook for the Claibornes?"

Rosa-Maria lowered her voice. "Because if you are living in the house, Holt will finally have a chance to know you." Her expression softened. "Once he does, he will see for himself how wonderful you are."

Jessie felt her throat tighten with emotion. Aside from

her best friend, Jorie, her grandmother was the only other person who knew of her feelings for Holt. The thought of moving into the ranch, of seeing Holt every day, filled her with a mixture of joy and terror.

"I don't know." She hesitated. "I'm not sure that's such a good idea, *abuela*. What if it doesn't work out?"

"Then at least you'll finally know. That's why it's not just a good idea, it's a great idea," Rosa-Maria insisted. "How else will you have an opportunity to see the real Holt? To get to know him on a personal level?"

Jessie dragged in a deep breath and blew it out slowly, considering. What if she did move in, but nothing changed in their relationship? What if she discovered he wasn't anything like she had imagined? What if he was even more, but she couldn't make it work?

"But won't Gus object to my moving in?" she asked. "You've been the cook and housekeeper at Riverrun for so long, maybe they won't want someone else stepping in, even temporarily."

"You leave Gus to me."

"What about Dad? He won't like me leaving the restaurant."

"It's long overdue. He'll get used to it." Her grandmother squeezed her fingers. "If you want to start your own business, now is the time to do that. He'll realize the restaurant will operate just fine without you there."

Jessie nodded, a frisson of anticipation tickling along her spine. "Okay, I'll try it for a month." She drew in a deep breath. "If I can't make it work after a month, then I'll call it a day and move on."

"That's my girl. Make him realize what's in front of him. And if it doesn't work, you need to live your life without him." Her eyes briefly closed and her grip on Jessie's hand slackened. "Don't let him fool you with his moods. He just needs a good woman . . ." Her voice trailed off as her eyes closed once more.

"*Abuela*, you're exhausted." Releasing her grandmother's hand, Jessie pressed a kiss against her cheek. "Sleep now."

Rosa-Maria opened her eyes. "Send your father and Gus in first. You're not the only one with a plan."

Jessie would have argued, but she recognized the glint in her grandmother's eyes. Rosa-Maria wouldn't allow herself to rest until she'd had her way and everything was settled to her satisfaction.

"Okay, then. Let's do this."

"HERE THEY COME," Evan said.

Holt lifted his head and watched as his father, Jose, and Jessie walked back toward the waiting area. Jessie looked more composed than she was when she'd arrived, thank God. He could handle anything except her tears. He rose to his feet and shoved his hands into his pockets to prevent himself from reaching for her.

"How is she?"

Jose nodded. "She's good. Tired, a little scared, but she's going to be okay."

"She's sleeping now," Jessie said. "Papa is going to stay with her tonight."

"What about the cantina?" Luke looked at Jessie. "Do you need to go back and help close up?"

"I called in some reinforcements," Jose said. "They have everything under control. Jessie won't be returning to the cantina."

Holt frowned and looked expectantly at Jessie, but she shifted her gaze to her feet and refused to look at any of them. "Everything okay?"

Gus gave a humorless laugh and pinched the bridge of his nose. "Here's the thing, boys. Rosa-Maria has decided it's time to retire."

"What?" exclaimed Evan. "I thought you said she was okay?"

Gus raised a hand. "She is, but even if she wanted to return to Riverrun, she needs time to recuperate. She can't be running around cooking, cleaning, and waiting on us. You heard the doc. She needs to slow down."

"Okay," Evan said. "So what are we talking, a couple of weeks? A month, at most?"

"My mother deserves a break," Jose said, his tone bordering on defensive. "She's sixty-three years old. She's worked for your family for twenty-five years and she's loved every minute of it. You've been very good to her. But now she wants a home of her own to relax in." He looked at his daughter. "Spend more time with her family."

"What she needs is a vacation," Evan declared. "But she can't *retire*. Like you said, she's only sixty-three. Once she feels better, she'll realize Riverrun is her home. That's where she belongs."

Holt watched his younger brother, understanding how he felt. Rosa-Maria had come into their lives when they'd been motherless young boys and they'd adored her from the first day. Her departure would leave a huge void in their lives.

"She'll always have a home at Riverrun," Gus said. "But if she wants to retire, no one is going to tell her she can't."

"She could take the foreman's cabin," Luke suggested. When they all turned to stare at him, he shrugged. "Why not? Jorie and I will be moving into the new house as soon as it's finished, so the cabin will be empty. It's perfect for a single person. Obviously, she can't stay at the main house."

"Why not?" Evan demanded.

Luke laughed. "Because all it would take is one day living with you Neanderthals, watching you struggle to fend for yourselves, and she'd be back to cooking your meals and washing your britches."

Evan's face cleared. "You're right! That's an excellent plan! We'll tell her she can stay in the main house for as long as she wants."

"She'll stay with me and my wife until she's better," Jose said firmly. "After that, I think we can let her decide where she wants to live."

"Quite right, Jose." Gus glanced at his watch. "Well, it's getting late and there's nothing more to be done here tonight. Jose, is there anything you need before we leave?"

"No, thanks," Jose said. "But maybe you won't mind

giving Jessie a ride home?"

"Of course," Gus replied.

"I'll drive her," Holt said.

Five pairs of eyes turned to stare at him in surprise. Holt was surprised too. He hadn't known he was going to make the offer until the words were out of his mouth, and then it was too late to pull them back.

"I have my truck and like you said, it's getting late," he said lamely. "You should go home and get some rest, Dad. I don't mind driving her home."

"Is that okay with you, Jessie?" Gus asked.

Jessie was still staring at him, looking a little dumbfounded. "Uh, yes, that's fine. Thank you, Holt."

"Sure." Clapping his hat onto his head, he shook Jose's hand. "Give Rosa-Maria my best when she wakes up. I'll be back tomorrow to see her. Good night."

He turned toward the exit without waiting to see if Jessie followed him, aware of her hurried farewells. Then she was stepping quickly after him as he made his way out of the hospital and across the parking lot.

"Could you maybe slow down a bit?" she called from behind him.

Holt shortened his stride, allowing her to catch up.

"I thought you drove over here with your brothers," she said, glancing at him.

"Nope. They won't ride with me and there's not enough room for the three of us in Evan's truck, so I drove myself."

They had reached his pickup truck and Holt opened the passenger door for Jessie, standing back as she pulled herself into the cab. Even so, he caught the tantalizing scent that he always associated with her—cinnamon and warm spices. He wanted to inhale her. Closing her door, he rounded the front of the truck, aware that she watched him through the window. He could kick himself for offering her a ride home.

He wasn't unaware of her feelings toward him, but he'd always been careful not to encourage her or give any indication that he noticed her efforts to catch his interest. She was Rosa-Maria's granddaughter, after all, and his sister Emmaline's childhood friend. She wasn't the kind of woman who did casual hookups, and he wasn't in the market for a wife. If he pursued any kind of relationship with her, he'd end up hurting her and the ripple effects would cause a rift between the two families. No way would he be responsible for that.

Jessica Montero was off-limits and it was best for everyone if he kept his distance.

Pretending he wasn't attracted to her was the hardest thing he'd ever done, but he willingly put himself through that torture every Thursday night at the cantina just to see her. Settling himself behind the wheel, he turned the ignition and eased the truck out of the parking lot and onto the main road.

"Why won't your brothers ride with you?"

He reached an intersection and brought the truck to a full stop, before accelerating through. "Because I'm a good driver."

To his surprise, Jessie laughed. "Oh, okay. By that, I take it to mean you're a slow, overly cautious driver. I can see why that would make Evan a little nuts."

Holt scowled. She made him sound like a decrepit old man. "I'm a safe driver, not slow. I won't put lives at risk just to get somewhere five minutes quicker."

"Well. That's very commendable."

Holt slanted a swift look in her direction. She was looking straight ahead, but even in the dim light of the cab, he could see the smile on her face.

"What?" he demanded. "Why are you laughing?"

She shook her head, schooling her expression. "I'm not. Really. It's just that—"

"Go on."

She glanced at him. "Emmaline told me you're very *responsible*."

Holt couldn't prevent the scoffing sound of disgust that escaped him. He wasn't unaware of his reputation as being dependable. Reliable.

Boring.

"You say that like it's a bad thing."

"No," she protested. "Not at all. I respect that about you, but don't you ever want to . . . I don't know . . . let loose a little?"

Holt took his eyes from the road long enough to give her a steady look. "No."

"Hmm."

That one small utterance carried a wealth of meaning. Holt's hands flexed on the steering wheel and he resisted the urge to defend himself. The truth was, he'd let loose once and what had it gotten him? A two-timing wife, an ugly divorce, and near bankruptcy. If not for his maternal grandfather, he might never have recovered from the financial loss.

Holt's mother had been the only child of oil magnate Charles Blaisdell and his wife, Grace. Growing up, Holt had been close to his grandparents and had spent most of his school vacations at their home in Dallas. He'd known they were wealthy, but he hadn't known just *how* wealthy until after they were gone and he'd inherited his grandfather's fortune. That had been three years after his messy divorce. If his ex-wife had realized he'd one day come into a substantial amount of money, would she have stayed with him? Thankfully, he'd never know. But if that experience had taught him one thing, it was to keep his private life that—*private*.

He'd invested most of the money he'd inherited, using a portion of it to start his cattle-breeding business with Emmaline's fiancé, Cort Channing. Beyond that, Holt didn't think much about his wealth. He lived a simple life, like his grandfather had. The money he'd acquired was incidental to his interests in running the ranch and raising cattle. He refused to let it define him.

So if he chose to live a risk-averse life, he had his reasons. And the biggest risk of all would be to *let loose* and give in to the overwhelming attraction he felt for Jessica Montero. She was the kind of woman you married, and he'd sworn never to go down that road again. No matter how much she appealed to him.

"Here we are," he said as he turned down the gravel road that led to her house.

Jessie lived in a small, one-story cabin on the banks of the Pedernales River, about three miles beyond the Claiborne ranch. One of several cottages that were popular with the summer tourists, it stood on wooden pilings and had a wide deck that faced the water. Pulling up to the house, he shifted the truck into park and rested his hands on the steering wheel. A motion light on the corner of the house came on, illuminating the deck and the riot of colorful blooms that spilled from the flower boxes. He could see several comfortable outdoor chairs and a small table on the deck, and wondered if she ever entertained there, and with whom.

"Thanks for the ride," Jessie said. "And what my grandmother said about retiring—"

"She's right," Holt said. "She deserves to spend the rest of her life enjoying herself. If we sounded less than enthusiastic, it's only because we've come to depend on her for so much. But we'll figure it out."

"Well, that's just it," she said. "You don't need to figure anything out."

Holt slanted his head to look at her. In the dim light of the dashboard, he could see her chewing on her lower lip, and her expression looked both hopeful and apologetic. Alarm bells went off in his head. "Why do I get the distinct feeling I'm not going to like what you're about to say?"

"It doesn't matter if you like it or not," she countered. "Because the decision has already been made."

"What decision?" Holt asked, but a part of him already knew what she was going to say.

Jessie smiled brightly. "Beginning tomorrow, I'm your new housekeeper and cook."

Chapter Three

JESSIE ARRIVED EARLY at Riverrun Ranch the following morning to pack up some clothing and other belongings that her grandmother had requested. But before she did that, she made her way to the expansive kitchen and set the coffee pot to begin brewing in two hours, which was when the Claiborne men typically sat down to eat breakfast together. That was just one of the things she admired about them; they seemed to genuinely enjoy each other's company and they always had each other's backs. She popped the egg and sausage casserole that she'd prepared the night before into the oven and set the timer. She'd discovered enough fresh fruit to put together a fruit salad, which she placed in the fridge. Then she quickly set the table and made her way to Rosa-Maria's apartment.

With its own separate parking and entrance, the apartment had a comfortable living area and kitchenette, with an adjoining bedroom and bath. The space had been added after Emmaline was born, in order to accommodate a live-in nanny. Emmaline's mother, Natalie, had been raised in the Hudson Valley region, just outside of New York City, and apparently au pairs had been all the rage. She'd insisted on having one for Emmaline and the boys, and Gus had indulged her by building the addition. But while the apartment had lasted, the marriage, unfortunately, had not. Following his divorce from Natalie, Gus had hired Rosa-Maria as a housekeeper and cook for himself and his children, and she had moved into the apartment when the boys were young.

Jessie could have remained in her own house rather than moving into the apartment, but that would have defeated the purpose of agreeing to take the job in the first place. She planned to insert herself into Holt's life as much as possible and living at the house would make that easier. Gus had agreed that having her live at Riverrun Ranch, even for just a month, made sense, but Jessie thought he would have agreed to anything Rosa-Maria had asked of him.

Being in Holt's house felt a little surreal. For the first time ever, she wasn't here to see his sisters or her grandmother. She was here to see *him*. To get to know him on a personal level. To hopefully make him notice her and maybe even want to get to know her better too. Stepping back from Rosa's Cantina would also make her father realize he could run the restaurant without her. She enjoyed working at the cantina, but she had a dream of owning her own food truck and serving authentic Mexican street food at the local festivals and rodeos.

Her father disapproved of her plans. He thought she should continue to work at the cantina until he retired, but he was only in his midforties so that day was literally years away. Jessie didn't want to wait any longer to get her Mexican food truck business up and running. She had her eye on a secondhand truck and would soon have enough money saved to purchase it. Her father might scoff at the idea of selling Mexican street food in such a small community, but Last Stand drew plenty of tourists and had more than its share of festivals and rodeos. And she was nothing if not determined.

She would make this work.

It didn't take long for Jessie to pack up her grandmother's clothing and the few personal items she had requested, including a small collection of photos. One picture, in particular, caught Jessie's attention. The photo was of Holt and his brothers when they had been little boys. She guessed Holt would have been no more than ten years old, and the twins looked to be about six or seven. Holt stood with an arm slung around each of his brothers' narrow shoulders, but while the twins were laughing into the camera, Holt's expression was one of almost adultlike seriousness. His hair had been lighter then, almost blond, but the volatile blue eyes hadn't changed, staring into the camera with an intensity that belied his age.

Jessie sighed, her heart aching for the boy he had been. She wrapped the photo in bubble wrap before placing it alongside the others. Picking up the box, she was preparing to carry it to her car when she heard masculine voices from the main part of the house and realized the Claiborne men had returned. She hadn't seen anyone when she'd arrived at six o'clock that morning, but that hadn't surprised her. Gus and his sons were typically up before dawn to take care of chores before they returned to the house for breakfast.

Setting the box down, she made her way through the main house and toward the kitchen to ensure the breakfast casserole had finished cooking. She heard Holt's voice first, and his words made her pause in the hallway outside the kitchen.

"Do we really need a full-time cook?" He sounded doubtful. "We're grown men. I think we can fix our own meals."

"Speak for yourself," Evan retorted. "Do you smell that amazing aroma? That's your breakfast cooking. Jessie did that, for us. What were you planning to eat? Granola?"

"I appreciate that she came in and prepared breakfast for us," Holt said. "But she has her own life; she doesn't need to spend it waiting hand and foot on us."

"It's already been decided," Gus interjected. "For the foreseeable future, Jessie is our new housekeeper and cook and there's no more discussion on the issue."

Holt made a sound that could only be described as frustration. "If you're so determined to have someone do the cooking and cleaning, fine. I won't argue. But why does it have to be *her*?"

Despite his mild tone, Jessie was momentarily taken aback. Did Holt really dislike her so much? What had she ever done to earn such hostility? Gus, apparently, had similar thoughts.

"What has that young woman ever done to you, son?"

"Not a thing, and I have nothing against her," Holt said. "I just think it's unfair to expect her to leave her job and her house to come work at the ranch. The position suited Rosa-Maria, but Jessica will be bored to tears out here. She's accustomed to working in a busy restaurant; this is just us guys."

"Maybe's she's looking forward to a change in scenery," Evan countered.

"We made Rosa-Maria a promise," Gus replied.

"What kind of promise?"

"She refused to retire unless Jessie filled in for her." Gus paused. "She was adamant about it."

Evan gave a rueful laugh. "And you agreed? We could have had Rosa-Maria back here in just a few weeks if you'd refused."

"Is that really what you want?" Gus sounded appalled. "For Rosa-Maria to come back to work and risk another heart attack? No, she deserves to retire and having Jessie here makes sense. Our family knows her, she's trustworthy, and she went to culinary school, so she's an excellent chef."

At that moment, the timer on the oven went off. Jessie didn't want to hear any more discussion about herself, so she drew in a deep breath and strode into the kitchen as though she hadn't just been lurking in the hallway, eavesdropping on their conversation.

"Good morning," she said brightly. "I hope you're hungry. I made an egg-and-sausage casserole for you."

They each mumbled a good-morning and cleared a path for her as she turned off the oven and grabbed some potholders. Holt moved to the other side of the large kitchen island, and Jessie was aware of him watching her. But when their eyes met, he abruptly turned away to refill his coffee. Jessie pulled the casserole out of the oven, checking that it was cooked through before carrying it over to the table. One of the ranch dogs, Sam, lay beneath the table and now he lifted his head, his nose twitching.

"Wow, Jess, that smells amazing," Evan said with appreciation.

"Thank you. Why don't you sit down and I'll get the rest of the breakfast together?"

Luke entered the kitchen from the back terrace, with Elsa at his heels. With a single hand gesture from him, the German shepherd lay down and rested her muzzle on her paws, her dark eyes never leaving Luke. He set his hat down on the island as his gaze swept the room. "Morning, Jess," he said. "I didn't see your car."

"I parked on the other side of the house. I packed up some things for my *abuela*," she said, taking the fruit salad out of the fridge and placing it on the table alongside a pitcher of orange juice. Rosa-Maria had made biscuits and gravy the day before, and now Jessie warmed the gravy in the microwave.

"Well, that's it," she said, when everything was on the table. "Dig in, and I'll be back in a bit to clean up."

"Why don't you join us?" Gus said, indicating the chair next to his own.

"Oh, no, I couldn't," she protested, even as her stomach rumbled.

"Rosa-Maria would eat with us sometimes," Evan said, as he sat down and reached for a biscuit. "I don't see why you can't do the same."

Still, Jessie wavered. She didn't want to set a precedent and Holt's words still rang in her ears. *Why does it have to be her?* She knew when she wasn't welcome.

"Have a seat, Jessica," Holt said and pulled out a chair for her. "You need to eat, and if your casserole tastes half as good as it smells, I guarantee there won't be any leftovers. Better grab some while you can."

Too surprised to argue, Jessie nodded. Holt rarely ever addressed her directly but when he did, he always called her Jessica. Never Jessie, or Jess. She liked that about him.

"Okay, if you're sure I'm not intruding," she replied.

"Not at all," Gus assured her, and retrieved another plate and set of cutlery.

They insisted she serve herself first and when she saw the enormous portions they helped themselves to, she understood why. There would definitely be no leftovers. They ate with gusto, clearly enjoying the food.

"Will you visit your grandmother today?" Gus asked her between bites.

Jessie carefully wiped her mouth. "Yes, of course. I spoke with my father earlier. He said they'll run some more tests today, but they expect to release her by the end of the week."

"So soon?"

"They assured us that with some lifestyle modifications, she should be fine. She'll stay with my parents, at least until she decides where she wants to live."

"I meant what I said about the cabin," Luke said. "Jorie and I will be out of there by the middle of next week, so she's more than welcome to take it for herself, for as long as she wants."

"I think that's a fine idea," Gus said. "She'd have her privacy, and we'd still be able to see her every day."

"Thank you, I'll let her know. But the final decision is hers," Jessie said. "She has some savings, so don't be surprised if she insists on paying a fair rent. If she even agrees to stay there, that is."

"I'm heading over to the hospital this morning," Gus said. "I'll convince her."

"And what about you?" Holt lifted his head to pin her with an assessing look.

"What about me?"

"Are you sure you want to stay here?"

Jessie found herself momentarily disconcerted by the question, but she was prepared. Staying at the house was essential to her plan, so instead of letting him see her flustered, she gave him a bright smile, reminding herself that she'd dealt with worse customers.

"Absolutely. I think it makes sense, don't you?"

Holt's brow creased into the frown she was becoming so familiar with. "Your house is just a few miles away. Wouldn't you be more comfortable there?"

"Maybe. But it's more convenient for me to stay here, especially if I'm preparing breakfast every morning." She poured herself a glass of orange juice and glanced at his set features. "Relax, cowboy. I'm not moving in permanently, if that's what's worrying you. And I promise not to tell anyone if you have weird bachelor habits."

Evan smothered a laugh.

"I'm not *worried*," Holt said, but a glint of curiosity had entered his eyes. "What kind of weird habits do you think I might have?"

Jessie shrugged and rounded her eyes at him over the rim of her juice glass. "I don't know. Maybe you wear bunny slippers in the morning, or you drink milk straight out of the carton."

She noted with relief the humor that curved his wide mouth. He took a forkful of casserole. "No bunny slippers in my wardrobe and as far as drinking from the container— you've got the wrong brother."

"Hey, no fair," Evan protested, but he grinned unabashedly. "I'm only guilty if you catch me."

Holt washed down his last bite of casserole with a gulp of coffee. "So, you're here solely for the convenience?"

Jessie could have given him the truth—that she was there solely for him—but that would have to be her and her grandmother's secret, at least for now.

"Holt," Gus chided softly. "Jessie's going to think you don't want her here and I know that's not the case."

Holt set his fork down and leaned back in his chair, not taking his eyes from Jessie. His gaze held a hint of challenge. "I just don't think it's necessary for her to live here. We're a house of bachelors, Jessica. Sure you're up for this?"

There was a moment of awkward silence.

"Well," Jessie finally said, making a show of folding her napkin, "my understanding is that I'm here to *cook* and do some light housekeeping. But if there's going to be anything kinky involved, I'll have to ask for more money."

Evan gave a hoot of laughter and even Luke grinned. Risking a glance at Gus, she saw his blue eyes were bright with amusement. Only Holt looked less than amused.

"For starters," Gus said, before Holt could speak again, "this is what Rosa-Maria wanted. Moreover, I asked Jessie to stay here as a personal favor to me. She's making a huge sacrifice in agreeing to help us out, so the least we can do is make it as convenient for her as possible. Besides which, I find we're all better behaved when there's a female in the house."

"Great." Holt pushed back his chair and stood. Gathering up his dishes, he carried them over to the counter and deposited them into the sink before grabbing his hat from the hook and striding out the door, letting the screen door slam in his wake.

"Well," Evan amended wryly, "*some* of us are better behaved."

Jessie set her juice glass down. "Maybe he really does have bunny slippers in his closet."

Inwardly, she was mortified by Holt's rudeness, but she wouldn't let his father or brothers see how much his behavior impacted her. Rising, she began collecting up the rest of their dishes. Gus stood and forestalled her with one hand on her arm.

"I'll speak to him. I hope you know how much we welcome your presence here."

"Thank you, but you don't need to say anything to him. I can handle Holt."

Gus nodded. "Good. Well, I'll be in my office. Come see me if you have any questions about anything."

"Don't worry, Jess," Luke said after Gus had left the kitchen. "I'll have a talk with Holt."

"I'm really not worried," Jessie said. "I actually expected something like this, just not so . . . blatant. I'll say something to him when I see him again."

"That should be interesting." Evan snagged another biscuit before scooping up the empty casserole dish and carrying it over to the sink. "I'm sure he doesn't have an issue with you being here, Jess. Just stay out of his bedroom."

Jessie looked sharply at him. Had he somehow guessed her feelings about Holt? Worse, did he really think she was the kind of woman who would sneak into Holt's bedroom? She couldn't prevent the warm rush of heat that rose into her cheeks at the lurid images his words evoked. But Evan was already turning back toward the table to grab the fruit bowl and the butter dish.

"Why on earth would I go into his bedroom?"

Evan shrugged. "To get his laundry or change his sheets. He prefers to take care of his own stuff. He hates for anyone to do things for him that he can do himself."

"Ah, duly noted," she said, relief flooding through her. "He doesn't want anyone to see the bunny slippers. Got it."

"By the way," Evan added, "today is sheets-and-towels day."

"For everyone except Holt," Jessie clarified.

"Now you're catching on."

After Luke and Evan left, Jessie finished cleaning the

kitchen, thinking about the morning's events. She suspected that Holt's attitude toward her stemmed from a rooted wariness of women in general. It made sense, given his history, and she preferred that reason to the alternative—that he disliked *her*. He'd always been affectionate toward his sisters and she knew how much he loved Rosa-Maria, but she realized she'd never actually seen him with any woman outside his family.

Glancing at her watch, she saw she had several hours before she needed to think about preparing lunch. She'd already planned to make hearty BLT sandwiches and homemade chips, which wouldn't take any time at all. As she made her way upstairs, she passed Gus's office. The door was closed and she could hear his muted voice as he spoke on the phone.

At the top of the stairs, she turned instinctively toward Emmaline's childhood bedroom, where she'd enjoyed so many sleepovers with her friend. It had been years since she'd been in this part of the house. Opening the door, she could see the room bore little resemblance to her memories. Now it was a guest room, pretty and functional, but nearly unrecognizable as the girlish retreat she remembered. Closing the door, she continued down the hallway and opened the next door.

This must be Evan's room. Masculine clothing lay strewn over an armchair, while boots and shoes had been kicked carelessly into a corner. The bed hadn't been made and through an adjoining door, she could see the en suite bathroom was in disarray. She spent the next half hour tidying the room and putting fresh sheets on the bed, before gathering up the soiled linens and towels and carrying them to the laundry room, where she stuffed them into the washing machine.

At the end of the corridor, she found Gus's bedroom. Like the man himself, the room was neat and crisp and devoid of anything fussy or superfluous. It took her less than fifteen minutes to put fresh sheets on the bed and replace the towels in his bathroom. Someone—her *abuela*, most likely— had set a small vase of fresh flowers on his dresser and Jessie made a mental note to replace them before they wilted.

In the hallway, she eyeballed the closed door of the bedroom she'd not yet explored, knowing it must be where Holt slept. She chewed her lower lip, debating. Did she dare? Surely just a peek into his room wouldn't do any harm and he'd never know. She was consumed with curiosity about what that private space might reveal about him. The house was quiet. She was alone except for Gus, and he was safely ensconced in his study. Setting the laundry basket down in the hallway, she carefully turned the doorknob, opening it just wide enough to take a quick look inside.

The room was large, dominated by an enormous four-poster bed on the far wall with elaborately carved bedposts. The walls were covered in a deep-gray-patterned wallpaper and there was a longhorn cattle skull over the bed, although Jessie was grateful to see the skull itself was made of glossy-black wood. Two dark leather chairs flanked a small table near the windows, and the room's only concession to softness was a sumptuous white rug on the hardwood floor. There wasn't a bunny slipper in sight.

Jessie frowned, no closer to understanding Holt than she'd been five minutes earlier, except to note he was exceptionally tidy.

"What are you doing?"

The voice, coming from the hallway behind Jessie, startled her so much that she actually jumped. Closing the bedroom door, she turned to see her best friend, Jorie, watching her with a knowing smile.

"Oh, my goodness," Jessie gasped, putting a hand to her chest to quell her madly thumping heart. "You scared the life out of me!"

"Were you snooping in Holt's bedroom?" There was no censure in Jorie's voice, only amusement.

Other than her grandmother, Jessie had never told anyone about her feelings for Holt, except Jorie. They had been friends since middle school and together, they'd spent many nights at Riverrun Ranch, having sleepovers with Emmaline and Callie. Jorie was a veterinary technician and had operated a wildlife rehab center out of her mobile home until a year ago, when the house had burned to the ground. But the entire town of Last Stand had come together to raise money for her to get reestablished. She was engaged to Luke and together they had were building a beautiful house on the land she owned, along with a new wildlife rehab center and a canine-training facility, which Luke owned and managed.

"I wasn't snooping," Jessie said, indignant. "I never even stepped inside. I was just . . . curious. What are you doing here, anyway?"

"Looking for you. How is Rosa-Maria? I couldn't believe it when Luke told me. Are you okay?"

Jessie nodded. "Yes, I'm fine. Emmaline and I are heading over to the hospital this afternoon to see how she's doing, but my father has been with her since last night."

"Luke said you're filling in for Rosa-Maria," Jorie said, her gaze turning meaningfully toward the closed door. "Doesn't that give you carte blanche authority to go in and clean Holt's room?"

"I think his room is off-limits," Jessie replied, picking up the laundry basket. "Evan specifically told me that Holt prefers to take care of his own stuff."

"Hmm, I like that in a man," Jorie said with approval. "Luke is the same way, but I always figured it was because of his military background. Maybe Rosa-Maria didn't spoil them too much, after all."

Jessie laughed. "If I know my grandmother, she probably made sure they all learned how to operate a washing machine and a dishwasher. Except for Gus, I am definitely not going to spoil them. I'll prepare the meals and keep the house tidy, but that's it. I am not going to be Cinderella and wait on them hand and foot. Besides," she added morosely, "Holt made it crystal clear he doesn't want me here."

Jorie followed her down the hallway to the laundry room. "Why? Did he say something?"

Jessie shrugged, as she pulled the wet laundry out of the washing machine and transferred it to the dryer. "He asked why I'm staying in the house, instead of at my own place."

"What did you say?"

"I told him it's more convenient, but maybe he has a point. Maybe I shouldn't stay here, but I was really hoping to put some distance between myself and my family. When I'm home, my parents think nothing of dropping in. And now that I'm not at the restaurant . . ." She gave Jorie a meaningful look. "You know how my parents are, especially my father. If it's good enough for him, it must be good enough for me."

"Well, given the choice between your parents and my own, I'd choose yours every time."

Jessie stared at her friend, stricken. Jorie's own mother had abandoned her when Jorie was just eight years old. She'd been raised by her grandmother in a run-down mobile home on the other side of town.

"Jorie, I'm sorry," she exclaimed. "That was thoughtless of me. Of course I love my parents, but sometimes I feel like I have no room to even *breathe*. I just really don't want to work at the cantina for the rest of my life. But is that reason enough for me to move in here and make Holt uncomfortable?"

"Are you sure that's the reason you agreed to move in?" Jorie's eyes held a knowing glint. "Maybe living under the same roof is how you'll finally get Holt to notice you."

Jessie gave her friend an admiring smile. "Beautiful and smart! Actually, that's the plan. My grandmother thought it would be the perfect opportunity for me and Holt to get to know each other better, so I'm giving it a month." She sighed and let her shoulders slump. "But if this morning is any indication, I think he's going to avoid me."

Jorie chuckled.

"What?" Jessie demanded. "Why are you laughing? I don't see anything funny in any of this."

"Because it's so obvious why Holt doesn't want you under the same roof." Jorie grinned. "He's attracted to you, and it scares the hell out of him."

Chapter Four

HOLT RODE HARD across the fields, driven by some unnamable inner force. The herds of cattle lifted their heads and watched as he galloped past before resuming their placid grazing. Only when he reached the boundary of the Claiborne property did he rein in his horse. The morning had already turned hot, but he barely noticed. Beneath him, Chaos breathed in gusty snorts and his neck was dark with sweat. Turning the horse south, Holt rode slowly along the fence line until he crested a small rise. Below him, nestled against a line of trees and bordered by a pretty stream, stood Emmaline and Cort's newly built house and barn. Gus had gifted them the land when they'd announced their engagement the year before. The location was convenient, since Holt and Cort had recently gone into business together, breeding bucking bulls. Cort had inherited his grandfather's stock of prime bull seed and, with Holt's financial backing and experience breeding cattle, they hoped to introduce some of the best bulls in the industry.

Holt urged his horse down the hill toward the house and dismounted in the shade of a massive live oak, securing the reins to a low branch. In the barn, he retrieved a bucket of cool water and hung it where Chaos could access it, before he made his way to the house and banged on the door. Pushing his hat back on his head, he glanced around the property. Emmaline's car was parked near the barn, but there was no sign of Cort's pickup truck.

The door opened, and Emmaline smiled when she saw him. "Hey, what brings you out here? Cort headed to the ranch about ten minutes ago."

Holt and Cort shared an office inside the breeding barn at Riverrun, where they kept the precious canisters of stud seed and maintained the genetic records for the cattle they bred. In addition to working the herds of livestock, they spent a good portion of the day managing the breeding program and soliciting buyers. Cort would no doubt be surprised to find himself working alone this morning.

"Actually, I'm not here to see Cort," he said. "Is there coffee?"

"Always." Emmaline stepped back to allow him to enter.

After removing his hat, Holt hung it on a hook near the entrance, and followed Emmaline into the new kitchen. The house had an artistic vibe but also showcased Cort's more traditional, Texas style. He sat down at the kitchen island and watched as Emmaline filled a mug with steaming coffee and slid it across to him. Then she leaned back against the counter, crossed her arms over her chest, and waited. She had pinned her long, dark hair back into a messy bun and Holt could see smudges of paint on her hands. Emmaline had an artist's studio at the rear of the house and she sold her paintings to galleries in Austin, San Antonio, and New York

City, as well as locally in Last Stand.

"Were you working? I don't want to interrupt you."

Emmaline waved his concern aside. "It's fine. I was in a good place for a break. So, what's up?"

"You've heard about Rosa-Maria?"

Emmaline nodded. "Yes, of course. Evan called to tell me. I spoke to Jessie, and she and I are going over to the hospital after lunch."

Holt sipped his coffee. "When did you talk to her?"

"Oh, about an hour ago, shortly after you stomped out of the house."

"I didn't stomp out," he retorted, frowning. "I had work to do."

"Uh-huh." Her tone clearly said she wasn't buying it.

"Is that what she said? That I stomped out?" He'd behaved badly, there was no way around it, but at the time, he'd been too frustrated to school his reaction. He was so conflicted right now, he could barely stand his own company. The plain truth was he didn't want Jessica living in his house, cooking and cleaning like a damned maid. Sleeping under the same roof.

Tempting him.

But neither did he want her to leave. He was already anticipating dinnertime when he would see her again. His guilty pleasure. His private hell.

"No, Jessie wouldn't say a bad word about anyone," Emmaline said. "But she said you made it clear you'd rather not have her there. For what it's worth, I think the situation has merit. Jessie loves her grandmother and she doesn't want her to worry about you guys, so she promised to move in and look after you."

"Christ, we're not helpless. We can look after ourselves." Holt narrowed his eyes at his sister. "Did she actually say anything else?"

Emmaline pretended to consider. "I think she said something to the effect that you're entitled to wear bunny slippers if you want to." She cocked her head. "Does that make any sense to you? Because she wouldn't explain it, just started to laugh."

Holt felt his own mouth curve upward. "Yeah, okay. I'm not going to explain that one, either. Otherwise, did she seem okay? I'll admit it; I was an ass this morning."

"I think you hurt her feelings, Holt." She studied him for a moment. "Try to be nice to her."

"I am nice to her," Holt objected, throwing his arms wide and trying to look innocent.

"Then what's the issue? Why are you so opposed to Jess working at the house? She's a wonderful chef and, more importantly, she's a good person."

Holt dragged a hand over his face. No way could he tell his sister he had the hots for her friend. Emmaline would tell him to go for it because she didn't understand that for him, Jessica was off-limits. Forbidden.

"Why don't you like her?"

He snapped his head up. "Does she think I don't like her?"

Emmaline's mouth quirked. "Well, you can't blame her. With you, it's sometimes hard to tell."

"It has nothing to do with whether or not I like her," he protested. "But having her in the house isn't the same as having Rosa-Maria around."

"Hmm, that's true."

"Rosa-Maria has been like a mother to us, while Jessica is—" He broke off, realizing he teetered on the verge of revealing too much.

"Gorgeous and smart and—" Emmaline leaned across the island and lowered her voice to a conspiratorial whisper. "*Single.*"

Holt scowled at his sister. "She's also extremely *young.*"

Emmaline gave him a narrowed look. "Just how old do you think she is, Holt?"

He shrugged. "She has to be at least ten years younger than I am."

"She's twenty-six, almost twenty-seven."

"Okay, nine years younger than me. To put it in perspective, I was already married and running the ranch when she was still only thirteen."

"Well, she's old enough now to be married and have her own family. In fact, she's older than Callie, who *is* married and has a baby, and Jessie is only a year younger than me." She tipped her head and considered him for a moment. "But somehow, I don't think this has anything to do with her age. I think you're just not used to being around pretty, *eligible* women. When's the last time you went on a date, anyway?"

"Okay, that's my cue to leave," Holt said, unwilling to discuss his love life—or lack of one—with his younger sister. He stood up and took a last swig of his coffee. "Thanks,

Em."

She raised her eyebrows at him. "Sure, anytime. Good talk, Holt."

He snatched his hat from the hook and then paused by the door. "When you see Jessica, tell her I'm sorry. I didn't mean to offend her."

"Oh, no," Emmaline said, raising her hands as if to ward off the very suggestion. "I am not getting in the middle of this. Besides, an apology would mean more if it came from you, don't you think?"

Holt gave a grunt of assent, but as he untied Chaos from the tree and swung himself into the saddle, he felt even more unsettled than he had before he'd arrived at Emmaline's house. Of course, he realized that Jessica was an adult. A man would have to be blind not to see what a beautiful woman she'd become. And that was the problem.

He wasn't blind.

Not even close.

Returning to the ranch, he unsaddled his horse and then gave him some more water. After brushing him down, he released the animal into a nearby paddock. His dog, Sam, a yellow Labrador mix, rose to his feet from where he'd been asleep under a shade tree, and came forward to greet him, tail wagging.

"Hey, boy." Holt crouched down to rub the dog's face and neck. "Having a rough day?" Sam shook himself, sending dust and fur into the air, and Holt stood. "I know the feeling."

Inside the breeding barn, he found Cort already in the

office, working on his laptop. Their partnership was working out better than Holt had hoped. Cort was smart and he knew bulls. In addition to the canisters of prime stud seed he'd brought with him to their fledgling business, Cort had also used his connections within the bucking-bull industry to purchase seed straws from studs that showed huge potential. To date, they'd used the seed to artificially inseminate nearly fifty cows, but the calving wouldn't occur for another six months. Since all their breeding cows were on the same estrus cycle, they wouldn't breed any additional cows until the following spring. They were in a waiting mode until calving season.

"Morning, Cort. Let's check the weight on the pregnant cows this morning," Holt said, opening his own computer.

"On it," Cort said. "I also want to increase their nutrition, add a pound of cottonseed meal to their feed."

"Sounds good."

The cows were kept separate from the main herd, spending part of their time in the barn where their condition could be closely monitored, and released into a separate pasture each day for grazing. Holt was pleased with their progress and had high hopes for the calves they would deliver the following spring.

He checked his email and responded to queries. When he was through, he and Cort weighed and measured the pregnant cows, entered the data into the computers, then checked the statistics to ensure the animals were gaining appropriate weight. They made phone calls and ordered in supplies, and the morning passed quickly.

"Well, I think I'll head home and have lunch with Emmaline," Cort said, pushing his hat onto his head. "After that, I'm going into town to pick up supplies. Do you need anything?"

Holt looked up from the article he'd been reading. Normally, he would walk up to the main house and Rosa-Maria would have lunch prepared on the terrace. But today he found himself reluctant to return to the house. As much as he wanted to see Jessie, he wasn't ready to face her. He hated that he might have hurt her feelings. He'd never been good at expressing his own emotions, but he needed to apologize for his earlier behavior.

"No, thanks. I'll see you later," he said, and watched as Cort picked up his keys and left the office.

Holt returned his attention to the magazine, but raised his head when he heard Cort speaking with someone. Recognizing the second voice as Jessica's, he shot to his feet and looked desperately around the office as if he might discover somewhere to hide. And then it was too late. Jessie appeared in the doorway of the office, a tentative smile on her face. She looked fabulous in a pair of snug jeans and boots, paired with a rose-colored T-shirt that complemented her complexion. Sam had followed her and now he rubbed his head against Jessie's hip, his tongue lolling out as he gazed adoringly up at her.

"Hey," she said, and pushed her hands into the back pockets of her jeans. The movement caused her breasts to thrust forward and Holt quickly averted his gaze, pretending an interest in the article that had become nothing but an illegible blur. "I brought you some lunch."

Holt did look at her then. "You didn't have to do that. We usually come up to the house to eat."

"Well, your father is at the hospital and Evan came by earlier and grabbed a sandwich, saying he was heading out to the east pasture to check on the herds. Luke is over at Jorie's property, helping the contractor with the house, so it's just you." She lifted one shoulder in a half shrug. "I know how busy you are, so I figured I would save you a trip and bring your lunch down to the barn."

He remembered Emmaline's words. *Be nice to her.*

"Thanks. But I wish you hadn't."

He watched as she schooled her features into a sweetly pleasant expression, the way he'd seen her do with difficult customers at the cantina. It was just one of the things he admired about her, how she could keep her cool when he knew full well she was annoyed as hell. And right now, she was annoyed with him.

"Well, I did. I'll leave the tray here and if you don't want to eat, that's up to you. Bring it up to the house with you when you come."

She swung away and Holt closed his eyes briefly, mentally berating himself. "Wait. I didn't mean that the way it sounded."

Jessie paused and turned back around. "Really? How did you mean it?"

Holt spread his hands. "Only that you shouldn't have gone to any extra trouble. You work hard enough as it is and I don't want to make any more for you."

"Oh. In that case, thank you. Apology accepted." Then she smiled at him.

Holt wanted to tell her that he hadn't apologized, but her smile was doing funny things to him and he found he couldn't formulate his thoughts, never mind words.

"Come see what I have for you," she continued, and then she actually held out her hand to him, as if she really expected him to take it.

Not a chance.

His brain might have shut down for a nanosecond under the wattage of her smile, but there was no way in hell he'd touch her. Instead, he jammed his hands into his front pockets and nodded with his chin in the direction of the door. "I'll follow you."

"I hope you like it," she said over her shoulder. "My *abuela* said it's one of your favorites."

Holt couldn't guess what she might have prepared for him, as everything Rosa-Maria cooked became his favorite meal. He followed Jessie out of the barn, his gaze fixated on the seductive swing of her hips as she walked. She was taller than average, and curvy in all the right places, with a waist that seemed impossibly slender. Her long, glossy, dark hair fell loosely around her shoulders and, as they stepped out of the barn, the sunlight picked out the caramel highlights that ribboned through the thick waves.

"Here you are," she said, and led him to an outdoor table beside the barn, shaded by several trees. She had draped a checked tablecloth over the wooden planks and a large thermos sat next to a tray covered with a white dishcloth.

Lifting the cloth, Holt saw she had made him two thick BLT sandwiches on rustic bread, with hand-cut potato chips, spears of pickles, and a small dish of peach cobbler. She was right; this was one of his favorite midday meals. His mouth watered at the sight and he realized how hungry he actually was. Sam had followed them outside and now he lifted his nose in the air, sniffing appreciatively until Holt commanded him to sit. The dog did, but his hopeful gaze never left Holt and drool began to drip from his jowls.

"This looks good," Holt said gruffly. "Thanks."

He sat down, unscrewed the top on the thermos, and poured a liberal amount of iced tea into the single glass she'd included. Glancing at her, he realized she hadn't moved. Was she really going to stand there and watch him eat? Discomfited, he set the thermos down and indicated the empty chair on the opposite side of the small table. "Did you want to join me?"

She wouldn't accept; he'd only offered in order to be *nice.* He figured after the morning's debacle in the kitchen, he could afford to extend an olive branch, safe in the knowledge she would refuse and hightail it back to the house. And he wouldn't blame her.

"Well," she said slowly, clasping her hands under her chin and smiling at him in a way that was both alarming and endearing, "if you're sure you don't mind, then thank you— I would love to."

Holt stared at her, momentarily taken aback. He'd been so certain she'd refuse that for a moment he didn't respond. Then, realizing he was gaping at her, he recalled his manners and transferred one of the sandwiches to a napkin and handed her the plate with the remaining sandwich.

She took the seat opposite him, picked up the glass of iced tea he had poured, and took a sip. "Mmm, delicious. There's nothing better than sweet tea on a hot day, don't you agree?"

Holt tried not stare as she licked her lips, the pink tip of her tongue the most erotic thing he'd ever seen. She pushed the glass toward him and picked up one of the sandwiches, holding it with both hands and biting into it with relish. Holt stared, transfixed. She had a luscious mouth, and he'd be lying to himself if he said he hadn't had one or two fantasies about what she could do with those lips. How could someone make the simple act of eating a sandwich look sexy?

Delicately wiping her mouth with her finger, she raised one eyebrow. "Are you okay? You're not eating."

"No, I'm fine," he assured her, and quickly turned his attention to his meal. "I just got sidetracked thinking about . . . work."

"Your work," she repeated, and picked up a dill spear. "You mean inseminating the females?"

With his sandwich halfway to his mouth, Holt stopped and stared at her. She was slowly sucking on the end of the pickle and he didn't know if it was by chance or design, but the way her lips were wrapped around the damned thing made him go hard beneath the table.

"What?" She bit through the pickle and placed the un-eaten portion on her plate. "Artificial insemination. That's what you do, right?"

He swallowed hard and forced himself to focus. Was she deliberately trying to arouse him? "Well, yes, but that's just part of it. The actual insemination takes less than a minute, so while it's obviously an important part of the breeding process, it's not the whole story."

"Why can't they be bred the natural way, as God intended?"

"Because we're targeting specific traits and behaviors," Holt said. "Some of the bull seed we use comes from bulls who are no longer alive, but whose genetic makeup is desirable in producing a high-performing bucking bull."

Jessie nodded. "I understand, but it still seems so . . . impersonal. I mean, less than a minute?" She looked at him from under her lashes and Holt could have sworn he saw a dimple in her cheek. "Those poor girls are getting the short end of the stick, if you ask me."

Holt's mouth quirked and he bent his head to hide his own grin. He wouldn't tell her that the insemination "stick" was actually a foot long, or that unlike the cows, the bulls at least had a guaranteed happy ending. No way would he give her any additional details about the insemination process. The truth was, it was a tricky job that required both training and technical skill. So instead of replying, he picked up his sandwich and took a hearty bite, and then raised his head to stare at Jessie in amazement.

"What did you do to this sandwich?"

Resting her chin on her hand, Jessie gave him a triumphant smile. "Do you like it?"

"Let's just say Rosa-Maria never made a BLT like this

one." In case she was in any doubt as to just how much he was enjoying the sandwich, he took another bite, unable to prevent the sounds of appreciation that escaped him. "This might be the best thing I've ever eaten, besides your carne asada. What did you put in this?"

Jessie watched him with undisguised pleasure. "Thank you, but it's just a BLT with a twist. I used fried green tomatoes, applewood bacon, and a secret remoulade sauce."

"And you made the chips from scratch," he said, eyeing the pile of curly, golden chips.

"I did. They have a dusting of spice on them. I hope you like them."

Holt tried one, tasting the faint hint of cayenne pepper. "They're delicious."

Holt couldn't recall the last time he'd been with a woman—a young, beautiful woman—who seemed to genuinely enjoy his company. He tended to avoid the opposite sex, unless they were family. Even now, suspicion lurked at the back of his mind like an insidious afterthought. Why would Jessica Montero want to spend any time with him? He'd been bad mannered and had made it clear he didn't want her around. Beyond that, he was nearly ten years older than her. Why wasn't she with one of the good-looking, brash young cowboys in town? He'd bet she had no shortage of guys knocking on her door. He steered his thoughts to safer territory, because he didn't like thinking of Jessie like that. He didn't like thinking of her with any other man, even if he couldn't imagine her with himself.

"So, the remoulade is a secret, hmm?"

"A family recipe, passed down from generation to generation," she confirmed, but the gleam in her dark eyes told him she was only partly serious. "No one outside the Montero family will ever be privy to the ingredients that go into that sauce. Not even if they beg."

"I never beg." Holt took another bite. The flavor was robust and savory, with enough bacony goodness to satisfy even him.

"That's too bad," she murmured. "For you, I might make an exception."

Her words, combined with the invitation in her eyes, nearly caused Holt to choke on his sandwich and he swallowed quickly.

"Well, I should get back." She took the last bit of her sandwich and held it out to the dog, who wolfed it down. Then she pushed the plate with the remaining half toward him. "Why don't you finish this? I've had plenty."

She stood, smoothing her hands down the front of her top and drawing Holt's unwilling attention to her slender waist above the gentle flare of her hips. He didn't want her to go, but could come up with no good reason for her to remain. He rose to his feet.

"Thank you. I'll bring the tray up to the house later."

"Thanks," she said, smiling up at him. "I'll see you at dinner."

Holt wondered if she had any idea how appealing she was, or if she had the slightest inkling of his true feelings toward her. She'd been nothing but accommodating and kind to both him and his family, and he'd acted like a surly jackass. As she turned away, he called her name.

"Jessica."

She spun back around, her expression both surprised and expectant. "Yes?"

"About this morning—"

She held up a hand. "Please, don't apologize. I understand."

Holt almost laughed, because there no way she could possibly understand. Worse, he couldn't promise that he wouldn't act like an idiot again. Having her under the same roof made him feel restless and edgy. But for her sake, he'd make an effort to be nice.

Holt watched as she turned and made her way back toward the house, admiring the perfect curve of her rear beneath the well-worn denim. When she had gone, he looked at the half sandwich she had left untouched, and picked it up. Biting into it, he was struck again by the unique flavors. She'd said the secret was a family recipe and no one outside the Montero family would ever know the ingredients. Holt gave a huff of laughter, thinking it might just be worth breaking his rules and marrying her just to get the recipe.

Chapter Five

JESSIE PARKED HER Jeep Wrangler in the parking lot of the hospital and gathered up the flowers and magazines she had brought for her grandmother. At the reception desk, she spoke briefly with the nurse on duty.

"How is she today?"

"Her spirits are good, but the doc wants to keep her for a few more days, just to get her sugar levels down," the nurse replied. "But she's had lots of company, so I'm sure that helps."

"Is she awake?"

"Oh, I'd say so." The nurse smiled knowingly.

"Thanks." Jessie turned away, puzzled. What had that smile meant?

She walked down the corridor to her grandmother's room, but came to an abrupt stop in the doorway before she stepped quickly back, out of sight. She stood for a moment in the hall outside the room with her back pressed up against the wall, astounded by what she had just witnessed.

Her grandmother was sitting up in bed wearing a pretty, flowered robe and Gus Claiborne was sitting in a chair pulled up close to her side. But that hadn't been what surprised her. Gus had been holding one of her grandmother's hands in both of his, gazing at her with undisguised longing and love. And her grandmother had been stroking his face with her free hand. As if they were lovers, and not employer and employee! The exchange had been so tender and intimate that there was no way Jessie could interrupt. As it was, she felt like a voyeur.

Turning silently away, she walked quickly back toward the main lobby, her mind reeling. Did anyone else know about the relationship? And how long had the two of them been romantically involved? Her grandmother was only sixty-three, just a few years younger than Gus. She'd been a widow for nearly thirty years, so there was no reason why she shouldn't have a man in her life, but Jessie had never expected that man to be Gus Claiborne.

"Hey, Jessie!"

She looked up to see Emmaline Claiborne walking toward her. Like herself, she carried a bouquet of flowers. She looked pretty in a summer dress paired with cowboy boots, with her dark hair loose around her shoulders.

"Emmaline!" They embraced awkwardly, laughing as they tried not crush their flowers. "Well, I don't think my *abuela* has any shortage of visitors today!"

Emmaline eyed Jessie's flowers and magazines. "Is she sleeping?"

Jessie took Emmaline's arm and steered her back toward the lobby. "No, she is definitely not sleeping, but I don't think you should visit her right now. She has company."

Emmaline frowned. "Okay, but I was really hoping to

see her."

Jessie laughed. "Trust me when I say you do not want to see what's going on in her room."

Emmaline stared at her. "Now I have to go see."

But Jessie hung on to her arm. "Let's go get a cup of coffee, and then we'll come back. Do you have time?"

"Here in the cafeteria, or downtown?"

"Let's go downtown," Jessie suggested. "We can go to Java Time and get a caramel mocha latte and you can tell me what you've been up to since we talked this morning." Seeing Emmaline's indecision, she added, "I promise we'll back within an hour."

"Okay," Emmaline said, and allowed herself to be steered away from Rosa-Maria's room.

Leaving their flowers at the reception desk, they drove together in Jessie's Jeep and found a parking spot directly in front of the coffee shop. It was late afternoon and downtown was fairly quiet, with only a few shoppers strolling along the covered sidewalks. Inside, they found a table near the window and placed their orders for lattes and two slices of chocolate cake.

"So why wouldn't you let me see Rosa-Maria?" Emmaline asked when their coffee and cake arrived.

"Because your father was visiting with her," Jessie said, sipping her coffee.

Emmaline shrugged. "So?"

Setting her coffee down, Jessie glanced around before she leaned over the table and lowered her voice so that only Emmaline could hear. "They were holding hands, and my grandmother was stroking your father's cheek in a way that was definitely not platonic. They looked romantic. I'm just glad they didn't see me. I think my mouth was hanging open!"

Emmaline's eyes widened. "Are you sure that's what you saw? Because that does not sound like the Gus Claiborne I know."

"Right?" Jessie sat back in her chair. "I can't tell you how surprised I was. She's never given any indication that she thinks of your father as anything more than a respected employer. To think that they actually have romantic feelings for each other is just—" She broke off, shaking her head. "It's crazy."

Emmaline leaned forward. "Maybe not. Sometimes it takes a near-death experience to wake you up to what's really important in life. Do you remember when Cort was stomped on by that bull in the arena last year?"

Jessie nodded. "Of course. Until we knew he was okay, it was awful."

Cort had been riding in the annual Last Stand rodeo and had been unable to escape the bull's hooves as he'd dismounted. The bucking bull had come down on his shoulder, breaking his collarbone, but to the horrified crowds in the stands, it had looked much worse.

"Exactly," Emmaline said. "For those few terrible moments, when I didn't know if he was dead or alive, I realized just how much I loved him and I regretted that I'd never told him."

"So, you're saying that my grandmother's heart attack

was a catalyst for Gus to admit his feelings for her?"

"Could be."

Jessie was silent for a moment. "How do you feel about that?"

"What do mean?" Emmaline took a forkful of chocolate cake. "We adore Rosa-Maria. If you ask me, they're perfect for each other. She knows his flaws and she hasn't headed for the hills. That's saying something. Besides, they've been alone for so long. They deserve to find some happiness."

"Hmm." Jessie was silent for a moment, considering her words. "Well, I hope I don't have to wait that long for someone to finally admit they love me."

"You do realize that you have to actually have a guy in your life in order for them to profess their love for you, right?"

Jessie smiled and dug into her chocolate cake. "I know. I'm working on it."

"Speaking of work," Emmaline said slowly, "why did you agree to cover for Rosa-Maria? I mean, you already have a full-time job at the cantina. Can your father spare you?"

Jessie wondered how much of the truth she could share with her friend. They'd known each other forever, but Emmaline was also Holt's sister. How would she feel if she knew Jessie and Rosa-Maria had concocted the plan in order for Jessie to spend more time in Holt's company?

"Well," Jessie replied carefully. "I told you how I want to start my own business running a food truck. I have the license and I almost have enough money saved for the truck. But my father wants to keep me at the cantina. He doesn't think a food truck will be successful. He's also convinced the restaurant will fail if I'm not there to help keep it running."

"Can't you do both?"

"Maybe, but not until after my business is established and I know what kind of sales I can make on any given day. Working at the ranch is the perfect opportunity for me to step back from the cantina. My father will finally see he can run the restaurant without me."

"So Rosa-Maria knew this?"

"Yes." Jessie smiled as she recalled the scene. "She said she would refuse to go to rehab and that she would come back to the ranch and risk another heart attack before she allowed some stranger to take over her duties. Both my father and Gus would have agreed to anything in order to calm her down, so when she said I was the only choice, they didn't argue." She paused. "And she also knows about my feelings for—"

She broke off abruptly, aware of what she had nearly revealed.

Emmaline paused with her fork midair. "Wait, what were you about to say? Are you in love with someone?"

"No! I mean, I definitely like this guy but I don't know him well enough to say I'm in love with him."

"Who is he?" Emmaline's eyes gleamed with anticipation. "No, wait. Let me guess. It's Evan, isn't it?"

"*What?*" Jessie burst out laughing. "No! Don't get me wrong, Evan's great but definitely not my type. He's way too casual for me and he never takes anything seriously."

Emmaline's eyes widened. "*Oh. My. God.* I don't know

why I didn't see it before." She leaned forward. "It's Holt!" Seeing Jessie's reaction, she sat back in triumph. "Ha. You don't even need to say anything, because I can see the truth written all over your face."

Jessie groaned. "Okay, I admit it. I've had a thing for him for as long as I can remember."

"How come I didn't know this? Why didn't you tell me?"

Jessie took another bite of cake as she deliberated how to respond. "Because you're his sister and that would be weird. Besides, I didn't want you to feel bad for me if he never returns my feelings."

"Everything makes sense now. He came by my place this morning and he was definitely out of sorts about what happened over breakfast. He at least recognized that he'd behaved badly, and he actually seemed concerned that your feelings might have been hurt."

Jessie sat up straighter. "He actually talked about me?"

Emmaline gave a rueful grin. "I think you were the single reason he came by. Don't get too excited, but I think you get under his skin, which is why it bothers him that you're staying at the house. You're too close for comfort."

Under his skin.

Jessie took another bite of cake and tried to quell her bubbling happiness. "I just wish I knew the best way to approach him. But he seems so conservative."

"Yeah, I think he's a little old-fashioned. Well, there's more than one way to catch a cowboy. Maybe you should start with your killer cooking skills. They say the way to a man's heart is through his stomach and nobody appreciates good food more than Holt."

"He actually ate something today that wasn't carne asada." Jessie grinned. "That's all he orders when he comes into the cantina on Thursday nights."

Emmaline put down her fork as if a thought suddenly occurred to her. "Have you ever stopped to consider why he comes to the cantina on Rosa-Maria's night off? There're plenty of other restaurants in town, but he chooses to go to the one where you work. Coincidence?" She dropped one eyelid in a conspiratorial wink. "I think not."

Jessie laughed. "Oh, come on. He barely even looks at me when he does come in."

"He's shy."

Jessie stared at her friend in disbelief, because *shy* was not a word she would ever use when talking about Holt. Emmaline managed to keep a straight face for several seconds, before she began to laugh. "Okay, okay, he is definitely not shy!"

"He's just . . . reserved," Jessie said in his defense. "Guarded. I think he's been hurt too many times."

"Well, when you consider that literally every woman in his life has walked out on him—except Rosa-Maria—it's not difficult to understand why he is the way he is." Emmaline gave Jessie a warning look. "But don't ever let him think you feel sorry for him. He would hate that."

"I've never felt pity for Holt, if that's what you're suggesting."

"He's such great guy. I've always hoped he'd finally meet

someone who could make him happy." Emmaline considered Jessie for a moment. "But the two of you are polar opposites."

"How so?"

"Holt is the epitome of control. I've only ever seen him lose his temper once and it scared the hell out of me. He's very conscientious. He thinks everything through to the smallest detail. He never does anything on impulse. You, on the other hand—"

Jessie waited. "Yes?"

"You do things based more on emotion and less on reason." Emmaline reached across the table and grabbed Jessie's hands, taking any sting out of her words.

"Is that a bad thing?" Jessie had heard the same criticism from her mother her entire life.

"No. In fact, it's one of the things I love most about you, because it shows how genuine and passionate you are. But it isn't something Holt is comfortable with. He's not going to know how to deal with it, so he'll do his best to avoid it." Emmaline paused and gave Jessie a meaningful look. "He's going to avoid you."

Jessie sat back. "I'm giving him a month to give me some kind of sign that he's interested," she confessed. "He's the single reason I agreed to work at the ranch. But if I can't make something happen in the next four weeks, then I'm throwing in the towel and moving on with my life."

"A month?" Emmaline asked. "And Rosa-Maria knows about this?"

"It was her idea, actually."

"I only had a three-day weekend with Cort, but it was enough. Granted, Cort's a little bolder than most guys but that's only because he's had to be. He's had to fight for whatever he's wanted so he's not the kind of guy to stand back and wait."

"Are you saying Holt is?"

"I'm just saying you might have to make the first move." Emmaline pulled a face. "Like you said, he's reserved."

Jessie polished off the last bite of her chocolate cake as she considered her friend's words. "Would that be wrong, considering I'm technically there as an employee of your family's?"

Emmaline's eyes glinted with gentle mockery. "Considering your reasons for being there in the first place, I'd say no."

"Well, *if* our relationship ever develops the way I hope it will and *if* Holt wanted a physical relationship, I would need to leave the ranch. Otherwise it would just be too weird." Jessie was anxious to change the subject. "Okay, so what do we do about my *abuela* and your dad?"

"If what you said is true and they have feelings for each other, I think Luke's suggestion to move her into the cabin is a good one. She'll still be on the ranch, but she'll have her own space and *privacy*." Emmaline waggled her eyebrows in a meaningful way.

"Okay, this is my *abuela* we're talking about," Jessie said, waving her hands. "I can't even go there."

Emmaline laughed. "I think it's wonderful. They both deserve to find happiness and if anyone knows my father's strengths and shortcomings, it's Rosa-Maria. If she agrees to move into the cabin, they can continue to see each other every day."

"Are we really playing matchmaker?"

Emmaline lifted her coffee mug, her dark eyes dancing. "I think I may have found my new calling."

"Hmm. We'll see." Jessie eyed her friend's plate. "Are you going to finish that cake?"

With a laugh, Emmaline pushed the half-eaten cake across the table. "It's all yours."

Chapter Six

MOONLIGHT SLANTED THROUGH the window beside the bed and cast the room in silvery light and purple shadows. Holt lay against the pillows with his arms bent behind his head, unable to sleep. Sam snored softly on his dog bed in the corner. On the wall over Holt's head, the longhorn skull seemed to stare balefully down at him. Why had he let Emmaline talk him into letting her decorate his bedroom? Because while building her new house with Cort, she'd also discovered a passion for interior design and decoration. Her enthusiasm had been infectious and when he'd casually mentioned that he wanted to redo his room, she'd offered to take it on herself. He hadn't had the heart to refuse her. She'd done a good job capturing his preferences in the masculine furniture and smoky tones, but the skull wasn't something he would have chosen. She'd been excited about the wall decor, but Holt reminded himself to take it down in the morning and replace it with something less macabre.

Glancing at his bedside clock, he saw it was after midnight. His alarm would go off in less than four hours and he'd be dragging his ass by noon if he didn't get at least a few hours of sleep. But damned if he didn't see Jessica every time he closed his eyes. She'd taken up way too much space in his head since she'd moved into the little suite at the back of the house. He still couldn't quite accept that the one woman who had the ability to distract and arouse him was sleeping under the same roof as himself. He'd had a thing for her since the night of her twenty-first birthday, but he'd kept his distance because he'd thought she was too young. In his mind, she was still young, but as Emmaline had pointed out, not that young. But what if she thought he was too old? Compared to her, he'd had a lifetime of experiences, not all of them pleasant.

Holt didn't consider himself to be an overly imaginative man, but whenever he closed his eyes, he could picture her as clearly as if she was asleep beside him in his oversized bed. In his mind's eye, she wore a white negligee that hugged her round breasts and barely covered her sweet backside, and her long, lustrous hair splayed out over the pillow.

He hadn't spent this much time thinking about a woman since his ex-wife, Alyssa, had dragged him through divorce court nearly ten years ago, and his thoughts then had been vastly different than they were now about Jessica. He'd met Alyssa during his last year at Texas A&M and he'd fallen hard. In retrospect, he realized he'd been vulnerable; susceptible to any female who'd shown an interest in him, and Alyssa had been *very* interested. Holt just hadn't realized she'd been more in love with his money than she'd been with him.

Jessica was different. Down to earth and wholesome, she

took genuine pleasure in family and friends. She'd never struck Holt as someone obsessed with wanting material things. More importantly, she seemed to enjoy living in Last Stand. Alyssa had hated his small hometown and had wanted nothing to do with Riverrun Ranch. She'd insisted on having an expensive house in Houston and another in Austin. Holt had worked for an investment firm during those years, and he'd done well, but no matter how much money he made, it hadn't been enough for Alyssa. There had always been something else she needed, wanted, or had to have, no matter the cost.

Pushing away the unpleasant memories, Holt flung back the sheet, sat up on the edge of the bed, and scrubbed his hands over his face. A light evening shower had damped down the warmth of the day and now a cooler night air wafted through the open window, stirring the curtains and raising goosebumps on his heated flesh. He needed a cold shower. Something—anything—to dispel the erotic images playing like a slow-motion movie in his head. Jessica Montero had gotten under his skin. He stood and as he did so, he heard a noise from downstairs that sounded like breaking glass. Sam raised his head and let out a low woof. Frowning, Holt opened his bedroom door and cocked his head to listen, but everything was silent.

He pulled a pair of jeans on over his boxers and without bothering to button them, made his way down the wide staircase to the first floor. Sam padded silently at his side. At the bottom landing, he paused, one hand on the dog's collar to hold him back. He could hear furtive noises coming from the kitchen and could see a faint, bluish light. What the hell? He might have thought there was an intruder in the house, but no one would be insane enough to burglarize the Claiborne ranch—not if they knew three Claiborne men lived in the main house.

Holding the dog to prevent him from bolting ahead, Holt made his way down the hallway until he reached the large kitchen. The noises continued, like the sound of glass being slowly scraped across the floor tiles and he could now see the source of the bluish light came from the open door on the refrigerator. Frowning, Holt felt for the wall switch and flipped it on, squinting at the sudden glare of light. He didn't see anything out of the ordinary, but then a figure slowly rose from behind the large center island.

Jessica.

Her hair was rumpled, as if she'd just rolled out of bed. Her eyes widened when she saw him and for a moment, she seemed at a loss for words. She stared at him, until Holt remembered he wore only a pair of unbuttoned Wranglers and no shirt or shoes. Releasing Sam's collar, he quickly fastened his jeans. But the instant he freed Sam, the dog gave a happy bark and barreled around the end of the island, his toenails sliding on the tiles.

"No, wait!" Jessie cried.

"Sam!" The dog immediately stopped and returned to Holt, his head down and his tail wagging furiously. "Good boy. Sit."

Assured the dog wouldn't move, Holt rounded the is-land. There, on the floor by Jessica's feet, glittering shards of a broken glass bowl lay scattered in a pool of melting ice cream.

"I didn't want Sam to get hurt," she explained. "Don't come any closer in your bare feet. Let me just clean this up." She flashed him a quick smile. "Now would have been a good time for those bunny slippers."

"You're barefoot too," he observed.

She wore only a snug tank top over a pair of loose shorts and her bare limbs were slim and toned and golden.

"But I'm betting I have more experience than you do in cleaning up broken glass. It's an occupational hazard at the restaurant." Even as she said the words, her breath hissed in and she grabbed at the island for support. "Maybe I spoke too soon."

"You okay?"

Lifting her foot, she peered at the bottom. "A sliver of glass, nothing serious."

"Here, let me take a look."

"Really, it's nothing."

But she didn't protest when Holt helped her onto a nearby stool. He took her foot in his hand and peered at the bottom, where a tiny shard of glass had sliced the arch. Her foot was slender and her toenails had been painted a shiny red. He tried not to look at the long expanse of her bare legs, but he heard how her breathing hitched the instant he touched her.

"Let me grab the first aid kit." Retrieving the kit from a cupboard, he removed the bit of glass, before applying a dab of antiseptic ointment and a Band-Aid. "There, all set. I think you'll live."

"Thank you, Doctor Holt." She smiled at him as he closed the medical kit. He was still crouched in front of her when, seemingly on impulse, she reached out and smoothed her fingers over his hair.

Holt froze.

"Sorry," she said, withdrawing her hand. "It's just that your hair is sticking up all over the place." Seeing his expression, she clambered quickly down from the stool. "I think I'll finish cleaning up the mess."

As she turned away, Holt groaned inwardly and pushed his fingers through his hair, trying to tame it. He watched as she deftly scooped the ice cream and broken glass up with the dishcloth, dumped the entire mess into the trash, and then made sure no glass shards remained.

"Here, let me help you." Holt retrieved a mop and quickly washed the floor, rinsed the mop and then went over the floor again until the last vestiges of sticky ice cream were gone.

"Thank you," she said when they had finished, surveying the floor with satisfaction. She glanced toward the door where Sam still sat obediently, his ears cocked, and gave Holt a meaningful look. "Someone has been very patient."

"Okay, c'mon over, Sam, I know you're dying to say hello." Released from his command to stay, the dog bounded toward Jessica and tried to jump on her. "Whoa, boy, down."

Holt blocked the dog from leaping on Jessica, but she bent forward and let Sam kiss her face. Holt watched as she scrunched her nose up and laughed.

"Such a good boy," she crooned, and rubbed behind his ears. "Yes, you are the best boy ever, aren't you?"

Holt told himself he wasn't jealous of the dog, but Sam's face was the picture of ecstasy. His eyes had closed to slits and his tongue lolled happily out of his mouth as Jessie stroked his head. She raised her head to look at Holt, still grinning, and he felt something catch in his chest.

This close, he could see her eyes weren't black, as he'd always thought. They were a deep chocolate brown and surrounded by lush lashes. Her nose was small and pert above full, pink lips, and her skin was warm and glowing. Holt swallowed hard and turned away to stash the mop back in the closet.

"I'm sorry I woke you up," she said behind him.

"Nah, don't be. I wasn't getting much sleep anyway."

"Me, either," she said. She pulled out a stool and sat down. "I remembered there was a container of butter pecan ice cream in the freezer and, after that, I couldn't sleep because all I could think about was how much I wanted some. So, I am not going back to bed until I've had my bowl of ice cream." She gave him an apologetic look. "I have an insatiable sweet tooth. Do you want to join me?"

Holt chuckled, surprised by her unexpected candor. "Sure. Butter pecan happens to be my favorite."

"I know."

Holt paused in front of the refrigerator and turned to look at her. "Really? How do you know that?"

Jessie bent down to pat Sam, who had come to sit at her

feet. She looked embarrassed. "My *abuela* mentioned it. I went shopping with her once and asked why she bought so many gallons at a time. She said she had to, because it disappears so fast."

Holt made a grunting noise as he opened the freezer. "We're a houseful of men. Everything disappears fast."

He withdrew a gallon of ice cream, pulled two bowls down from a cupboard, and began dishing out portions. When he finished, he put the container back in the freezer and slid one bowl across to Jessie. He didn't sit down but instead leaned against the opposite side of the island as he dug into the sweet treat.

"So why couldn't you sleep?" he asked between bites, not looking at her.

"Honestly?"

Glancing at her, Holt wasn't certain he wanted to know because he sensed he might be the reason. "Sure."

"I kept thinking about how you reacted at breakfast this morning, and how you so obviously don't want me here." She tipped her head as she considered him. "Why is that? Do you dislike me? Have I done something to offend you?"

Holt paused, his spoon halfway to his mouth, and stared at her. How would she react if he told her he didn't dislike her? That, in fact, the opposite was true? That he found her a huge distraction, to the point where he couldn't sleep because he couldn't stop thinking about her? That he'd been unfocused and frustrated, knowing she was in his house? No, he couldn't tell her any of that. She was forbidden fruit, no matter how tempting and sweet she might be. He set his bowl and spoon down and spread his hands on the island.

"I don't dislike you," he began. "Jessica—"

She leaned forward, her expression earnest. "Give me a month, Holt. That's all I'm asking. That will give my grandmother the time she needs to get better and it will give me time to—" She broke off.

"Time to . . . what?"

She retreated, focusing on her bowl. "Nothing."

But she'd piqued his curiosity. Clearly, she didn't want to tell him, which made him even more determined to pry it out of her.

"No, tell me. I'd like to know."

Jessie glanced at him and Holt thought she looked embarrassed. She pushed her spoon through her softening ice cream. "I have a plan, but I need a month or so to see if it works."

Holt took another bite of his late night dessert, intrigued. "Oh, yeah? What does this plan involve?"

Now there was no question she was uncomfortable. She was practically squirming on her seat. "You'll think it's ridiculous."

"So, tell me anyway. Maybe I can help?"

"I've been saving for a food truck. I've been approved for a license and I almost have enough money set aside to purchase the truck."

"A food truck," Holt mused. "How much do those cost?"

"The one I want is just over fifty thousand dollars. I could take out a loan and own it tomorrow, but I really want to get started without any debt."

"That doesn't sound so ridiculous," he said carefully. "You think you'll have enough money after a month?"

"I hope so, but that's not the only reason I came to Riverrun. My father disapproves of my plans and wants me to continue working at the cantina. The thing is, I've worked there since I was a teenager, and the cantina is his dream, not mine. He won't even let me cook because he thinks I'm going to change his recipes and drive away his loyal customers."

"You want your own business."

She cast him a grateful look. "Exactly. I have so many great ideas and I've tried to implement them at the restaurant, but my father is such a traditionalist. He doesn't want to take any chances, or do anything that might be risky. He refuses to put anything new or modern on the menu."

"Well, the carne asada is pretty spectacular just the way it is," Holt ventured. "Why mess with perfection?"

"Says the man who has ordered the same thing for the past five years." Jessie smiled at him. "One or two new items wouldn't hurt. Sometimes you just need to take a chance and try something different, even if it's out of your comfort zone."

Holt paused in the act of lifting his spoon. "Are we still talking about the restaurant?"

"What do you think we're talking about?" she asked, rounding her eyes in innocence.

Holt felt a reluctant smile curve his mouth. "I can have an open mind and take chances."

"Uh-huh." Her tone clearly said she didn't believe him.

"I'd like to see that."

"Would you really?"

The air between them turned heavy, weighted with awareness and anticipation. Jessie's gaze drifted downward, over his bare shoulders and arms, before lifting back to his face. She swallowed hard. "Yes."

The simple word sent Holt's heart careering. His very open-minded imagination took off with all the possibilities of how he could demonstrate his liberal leanings. Before he could respond, Jessie beat a fast retreat.

"Anyway," she said brightly, focusing on her ice cream, "this is an opportunity for me to step back from the restaurant and get my own business up and running."

With her attention no longer fixed on him, Holt found he could breathe normally again.

"Have you talked to your grandmother about your plans?"

Jessie looked at him. "Of course. She knows everything."

"Does she know you need money?"

Jessie recoiled. "I would never ask her for a loan, Holt. Anything she has, she'll need for her retirement. I can manage on my own."

Holt suppressed a smile. "Okay, forget I mentioned it. Do you think there's enough business in Last Stand to sustain a food truck?"

"I do think so. There's the Peach Festival and the Bluebonnet Festival, Cinco de Mayo, the Fourth of July parade and rodeo, and the Christmas festival. And that's just here in Last Stand. I could also attend festivals in surrounding areas—there's always a celebration of some kind going on. When there is no festival, I could set up near the park and sell Mexican street food from the truck. People could also hire the truck—and me—for special events, like birthday parties or graduations."

The words tumbled out of her, as if she was trying to convince herself rather than him that a food truck was a good idea.

"Mexican street food, hmm? My dad used to bring me to Mexico sometimes as a kid, when he would go to purchase cattle. I always loved getting street food." Holt thought the idea had merit. There were two Mexican restaurants in town, including the cantina, but Last Stand was a tourist destination and there were always people looking to eat something fast, affordable, and delicious. And everything Jessica cooked was amazing. She'd have no shortage of customers. "I think it's a great idea."

"You do?"

"It's never wrong if you're following your passion."

Jessie stared at him as if he'd said something outrageous. "What?"

"Nothing," Jessie said, shaking her head. "I guess I just thought—well, everyone except my grandmother is against the idea, so I just assumed you would be too."

"I'm not quite as old-fashioned and decrepit as you think."

Jessie laughed. "Trust me, I've never thought of you as decrepit."

The space between them was suddenly taut. More than

anything, Holt wanted to know what she did think of him, but he wouldn't ask.

Jessie pushed her bowl away. "Well, that was delicious. I should probably get back to bed. Morning will be here before we know it. I'll just clean up."

"Let me," Holt said, as she stood. "I'll throw the dishes in the dishwasher and no one will be the wiser that we were even here."

"Our secret, hmm?"

The conspiratorial smile she gave him was charming, making him suddenly wish they did have shared secrets. The unexpected longing hit him like a punch in the gut, because he'd vowed to never go down that road again. He wasn't sure he could ever trust another woman with his secrets. He'd learned the hard way that secrets could come back and bite you right in the ass. He'd been single for this long; another fifty years or so wouldn't kill him.

"Well, unless you want to take the blame for why we go through so much ice cream in this house," he said, trying to lighten things up, "we don't have to tell anyone about your midnight forays into the freezer."

She pulled a face. "I told you I have a sweet tooth. I can't promise it won't happen again." She paused. "You're always welcome to join me, though."

Holt was aware that most people thought of him as un-imaginative. Boring. They'd undoubtedly be surprised if they knew how her words impacted him. His head was suddenly filled with erotic images of her indulging in a midnight snack that had nothing to do with food—although some whipped cream wouldn't go wrong in this particular fantasy.

He needed to put some distance between them. No way would he tell her his inability to sleep had everything to do with her. That would fall into the category of giving her power. Nor was he sure he wanted to make a habit of meeting her for a midnight tryst. He'd end up sleep-deprived and even more sexually frustrated than he was already. He pushed the disturbing thoughts aside and gathered up the ice cream bowls.

"It's probably better if I don't make a habit out of this," he said gruffly, turning away. "But if anyone asks, I'll say I'm the one going through the ice cream, so feel free to indulge."

"Oh. Okay, well, thank you for helping me clean up the evidence," she said.

Holt stashed the dishes in the dishwasher and snapped out the light. "After you."

He followed her down the dim hallway to the bottom of the stairs, where she paused. Rosa-Maria's apartment was through the dining room, on the far side of the house.

"Good night, Holt," she said softly. In the dim light that streamed in through the windows, she looked seductive. Mysterious. "Thank you again."

"It was my pleasure."

He was unprepared when she leaned up and pressed a swift, soft kiss against his mouth.

"Sleep tight," she murmured, and she began to turn away.

"Jessica."

"Yes?" She spun back toward him and her expression

looked hopeful.

His hands went to her hips and tugged her closer, and his mouth sought hers again, brushing lightly over her lips. He told himself he'd back off if she gave any indication the kiss was unwelcome. Instead, she pressed in and wound her arms around his neck. Her fingers stroked his bare skin and Holt slanted his mouth over hers, seeking better access. She made a small noise and opened, and the touch of her tongue against his was electrifying. He gathered her closer, until he could feel the press of her soft breasts against his bare chest. He slid one hand to the back of her head, sifting his fingers through her long hair and cradling her scalp as he feasted on her mouth. How long they stood locked together in the scalding darkness was a mystery to Holt. It could have been mere minutes, but the erotic kiss seemed to go on forever.

When she finally pulled away, Holt found himself reluctant to release her. She held on to his hands and then leaned forward and pressed a single, searing kiss against the center of his chest, before she stepped back.

"Good night, Holt."

Before he could respond, she vanished through the doorway that led to the apartment.

"Good night, Jessica."

Holt climbed the stairs to his own bedroom, knowing he wouldn't get any sleep that night.

Chapter Seven

IGNORING THE NAGGING headache from a lack of sleep, Jessie managed to make her way to the kitchen the following morning in time to prepare breakfast for the Claiborne men. By the time they filed into the kitchen at eight o'clock, she had a heaping platter of breakfast quesadillas stuffed with fluffy eggs, bacon, cheese, and avocado and a skillet of crispy potatoes, accompanied by bowls of fresh pico de gallo and sour cream. Then, because Gus had a sweet tooth, she had also made sweet empanadas with a fruit filling, dusted with sugar.

"Ah, this all looks delicious," Gus said, surveying the table. "Thank you, my dear."

Despite his kind words, Jessie had the distinct sense that Gus was out of sorts and putting on a good face for her sake. There were shadows under his blue eyes that said something was troubling him.

"Is everything okay?" she asked quietly.

He pinioned her with a sharply assessing look and his smile grew wider, but Jessie thought it was no less artificial. "Of course! Why wouldn't it be?"

"No reason," she said hastily, wondering if her grandmother's absence had anything to do with his subdued manner. "But I think you should get more rest. I heard you in your office at five a.m."

Gus chuckled and it seemed more natural. "That means you've been up since five a.m., as well."

"Well, I had a reason to be up so early." She smiled. "But if you don't have to do chores, you should sleep in. You've earned it."

"Sleep eludes me these days, my dear. Forgive me if I don't eat at the table this morning. I have a lot of work to catch up on, so I'm going to have breakfast in my office."

"I'll put together a tray for you and bring it right in," Jorie offered.

"That's exactly what your grandmother would have done," Gus said wistfully.

Gus vanished into his office once more as Holt and Evan entered through the terrace door. Jessie's gaze slid to Holt as he poured himself a cup of coffee. He wore a Henley jersey with the sleeves pushed up over his strong forearms. The soft fabric emphasized the broad thrust of his shoulders and the planes of his chest, and Jessie recalled again how he had looked last night, when he'd worn no shirt at all. She could still feel the pressure of his body against her own, still taste him against her lips. As much as she'd tried, she'd been unable to find sleep after she'd left him.

Even now, the memory of that kiss caused her body to tingle all over. She couldn't stop thinking about all that hard, warm muscle, or the cobbled terrain of his stomach. The guy was supremely fit. Last night, she'd seen a side of him that she'd never seen before; a warm and humorous side. A tender, sexy side. Combined with his good looks, Jessie couldn't believe he was still single. He was the stuff fantasies were made of.

"Will you join us?" Evan interrupted her thoughts.

"No, not this morning," Jessie said, retrieving Gus's plate and heaping it with food. "I promised your father I would bring this in to him and then I have a few things to do."

Holt turned from the counter and their eyes met. His expression gave nothing away, but Jessie thought his eyes held a secretive smile, as if he was also thinking about the previous night.

"Good morning, Holt." She placed Gus's plate on a tray and poured a glass of orange juice. Retrieving two single flowers from the vase in the center of the table, she found a bud vase in the cupboard over the coffee machine and dropped the stems inside. As she filled the vase with water and placed it on the tray, adding a napkin and silverware, she was acutely aware of Holt watching her.

"Morning, Jessica. Sleep well?"

"Like a baby," she fibbed. She glanced at him as he walked past her, noting the beard growth on his jaw and the lines of fatigue around his mouth. Unless she was mistaken, Holt hadn't gotten any more sleep than she had last night.

"This looks fantastic, Jess." Evan served himself a quesadilla and loaded it with pico de gallo and sour cream. "Any chance I can sweet-talk you into grabbing me a cup of coffee?"

"Of course," Jessie replied.

But as she turned toward the coffee machine, Holt fore-stalled her with a hand on her arm. "Get it yourself, Evan." His voice was mild, but there was an underlying edge to it. "She's not a servant."

"Really, Holt, I'm right here and I don't mind," Jessie protested, pulling free and casting an apologetic glance at Evan.

"No, he's right. I can get my own coffee." Evan stood and crossed the kitchen to the coffee machine. He frowned at Holt as he passed. "What's eating you this morning, anyway? You've been as ornery as a pregnant mare with a horsefly on her ass."

Luke entered the kitchen in time to hear the exchange. Now he cast an amused glance at Holt. "He's operating on no sleep, is my guess."

"What makes you say that?" Holt grumbled, as he stepped away from Jessie and sat down at the table.

"As it happens, I also suffer from occasional insomnia. I saw the lights on in the barn around three a.m. and figured it was you."

"Oh yeah?" Holt dished some fried potatoes onto his plate. "But you didn't think to join me?"

Luke laughed softly. "No way. I know what you're like when you can't sleep. Besides, I had other . . . distractions."

Jessie turned away to hide her smile, guessing that Luke's "distraction" had been Jorie, finding him awake at three a.m. and pulling him back to bed to cuddle until dawn. But the realization that Holt had not slept, but had instead sought refuge in the barn, was fascinating news to her. Casting a furtive glance at him, she found him watching her across the kitchen with an expression that turned his blue eyes molten. For a moment, Jessie couldn't breathe. Then he turned his attention to his plate, releasing her from where she'd stood, frozen.

She lifted the breakfast tray but before she could take two steps, Holt was there, taking it from her hands.

"Let me get this for you."

"I can manage," Jessie protested.

"I'm sure you can, but for this morning at least, you don't need to."

Acutely aware that Evan and Luke watched them with sudden interest, she made a helpless gesture. "I cut my foot last night and it's a little uncomfortable to walk on."

As soon as the words were out of her mouth, she knew she'd been wrong to say anything. Luke and Evan exchanged a meaningful look and bent over their plates, but Jessie saw their knowing smirks. Holt had already vanished down the hallway and into his father's study, so Jessie turned back to his brothers.

"It's not what you think," she said in exasperation.

Evan shrugged, but his blue eyes danced with humor. "Hey, what you and Holt do at night is none of my business."

"So you're the reason he didn't get any sleep," Luke mused, and a deep dimple appeared in one cheek.

"Oh, you two are hopeless," Jessie grumbled.

She left the house and stood on the wide verandah, her thoughts churning. Seeing the porch swing at the far end of the covered porch, she sank onto it, pushing it into gentle motion with her uninjured foot. Sunlight slanted across the swing, warming her. Maybe coming to Riverrun Ranch hadn't been such a good idea, after all. Being in such close proximity to Holt was both heaven and hell, especially when he ran hot and cold where she was concerned.

"Hey, Jessie, I thought that was you."

Startled, Jessie looked up and saw Jorie standing on the lawn just below the verandah, shading her eyes with one hand. "Hi, Jorie! What're you doing?"

Jorie indicated her small SUV parked along the side of the long, gravel drive. "I was heading into town. Are you okay?" Without waiting for an answer, Jorie climbed the stairs to the covered porch and sat down on the swing next to Jessie. "How's the new job going?"

Jessie shrugged. "Okay, I guess. I mean, cooking for four hungry men is the easy part."

"Well, cooking has always been easy for you. What's the hard part, as if I don't know?"

Jessie groaned and gave her friend a helpless look. "Holt is sending such mixed signals. I'm so confused. I don't know whether he wants to toss me out, or throw me across the kitchen table and have his wicked way with me."

Jorie's hands flew to her mouth, before she grinned widely. "Are you serious? What happened? Tell me everything."

Jessie gave her a brief account, beginning with Holt's rudeness at the breakfast table the previous morning, and finishing with how she had kissed him good-night. By the time she finished, Jorie's eyes were wide and round, her mouth open in astonishment.

"And all that time, he wore nothing but a pair of Wranglers?"

"*Yes!* And when he first entered the kitchen, they weren't even buttoned." A gurgle of laughter escaped Jessie. "I thought I was dreaming."

"So romantic . . ." Jorie sighed dreamily. "Don't get me wrong; I adore Luke and I think he's the sexiest man on the planet, but I would have loved to have seen that!"

"After he took care of my foot, he mopped the floor," Jessie added. Her gaze slid solemnly to Jorie's and her voice dropped to a stage whisper. "Wearing nothing but a pair of Wranglers! Honestly, it was like watching porn."

They stared at each other for a moment, before they both burst into peals of laughter.

"I can't believe you let him go upstairs alone," Jorie said when she could speak again. "You had him right there, half-naked!"

"Oh, no," Jessie said, putting up one hand. "There was no way I am sleeping with him, at least not while I'm working there. Technically, he's a client."

"Gus hired you, so *technically*, you work for him, not Holt." Jorie leaned closer. "Were you tempted?"

Jessie recalled how Holt had looked in the semidarkness of the hallway, all sculpted muscle and glittering blue eyes, and felt heat rise in her cheeks. "Of course. But I'm also a coward. I don't know what I'd do if he rejected me."

"If he's being distant, it's probably because he's afraid. Luke said he avoids women like the plague."

Jessie didn't tell her friend that there had been nothing distant about Holt last night. In fact, she'd seen an entirely different side of him. "I don't think Holt is afraid of much. He's just being careful."

Jorie made a sympathetic sound. "How's your foot now? Maybe you'd like to come into town with me?"

"Thanks, my foot is absolutely fine," Jessie assured her. "But I have too much to do today to go anywhere. Sorry."

"What do you have going on?"

Jessie sighed. "Apparently today is laundry and ironing day." She gave her friend a weak smile. "This may be the end of my short tenure as housekeeper, because I can barely sort my own laundry, and I avoid ironing at all costs. The first time Mr. Claiborne finds pink boxers in his dresser or a wrinkled shirt in his closet, I'll be history."

"Why would you do their laundry?" Jorie looked perplexed. "They're grown men."

"My grandmother did this for them, so I think they expect me to do the same."

"Just because Rosa-Maria did it doesn't mean you have to," Jorie said, her tone emphatic. "In fact, I would take all the laundry, bundle it into separate pillowcases and take it into town to the cleaners. Then all you need to do is put it in their rooms, all nice and clean and folded."

Jessie stared at her friend. "You would?"

"Absolutely."

"I don't know why that never occurred to me," Jessie said. "Do you suppose I could get away with bringing someone in to clean the bathrooms and mop the floors?"

Jorie leaned forward. "You're a *chef*, not a housekeeper. If Gus had any sense, he would never have asked you to do all of those other things."

"He didn't," Jessie confessed. "This was my grandmother's idea, partly to help with the cooking and cleaning, but mostly to get closer to Holt."

"So let someone else do the heavy lifting. All you should do is the cooking. If you need the name of a good house cleaner, let me know." She stood up. "Listen, I'm sorry, but I have to go. I'm meeting Emmaline at the new house and I don't want to be late. She's doing the interior decoration and the movers are bringing some of the bigger pieces of furniture over today. Luke and I are planning to move in by next week, so the cabin will be empty if Rosa-Maria does decide to take it."

"Thanks, I'll let her know."

Jessie watched as her friend climbed into her car and drove down the long, gravel driveway. There was no reason why she shouldn't do exactly as Jorie suggested and have someone else do the laundry and the cleaning.

The sound of masculine voices drew her attention, and she turned to see Holt, Luke, and Evan leave the house and cross the lawn toward the barns. Holt was the tallest, but they each had the same easy, loose-limbed stride that marked them as brothers more than their looks ever could. She'd known the Claiborne family her entire life, but realized she didn't know the Claiborne brothers, not really. Holt had been so much older than herself that, by the time Jessie had begun to notice him, he was already a grown man. Luke had joined the army as soon as he'd turned eighteen and had only recently returned to Last Stand. Evan, the brother she knew best, was a charming ladies' man who seemed to breeze through life without ever taking anything seriously, most notably his numerous, short-lived relationships. She suspected there was much more to Evan than he let the world see, but it would take a special woman to break down the barriers he'd constructed around his heart.

She guessed the same might be said for Holt, too, considering every woman he'd cared about had abandoned him in one way or another. Did she have what it took to break through his walls?

She had just under four weeks to try.

Chapter Eight

"I AM NOT returning to Riverrun Ranch. I am officially retired," Rosa-Maria said firmly, holding a vase of flowers on her lap. "I'll stay with your parents until I am better and then I will find an apartment somewhere in town."

"But Gus said he wants you to have the cabin," Jessie said, holding her grandmother's hand as she and her parents wheeled Rosa-Maria out of the hospital and toward the waiting car. "Luke and Jorie have moved into their new home on Hickory Creek Road, and the cabin is empty." Seeing her grandmother's stubborn expression, she squeezed the older woman's fingers. "Well, just think about it, hmm? You've lived there for twenty-five years. I'm sure they all miss seeing you."

Nearly a week had passed since the midnight kiss in the hallway. Her grandmother had finally been deemed well enough to return home, but she had been adamant about not returning to Riverrun Ranch in any capacity, not even as a retiree. If Jessie hadn't witnessed that tender moment between Rosa-Maria and Gus in the hospital, she would have believed the two had had a falling out.

"How are you getting along at the ranch?" Rosa-Maria smiled at her. "Are the boys treating you well?"

Jessie slid a glance at her father, who stared straight ahead as he pushed the wheelchair. "I'm doing fine and everything is going well," she assured her grandmother, putting an emphasis on *everything*. "I've settled into a routine of sorts and I think everyone is happy."

Jose made a grunting sound and Jessie's mother, Gina, hushed him. "The Claibornes are very lucky to have you," she said to Jessie. "It was a very generous thing you did, stepping in when your *abuela* couldn't be there."

"You'd do better returning to the restaurant," Jose grumbled. "When I agreed to let you go, I thought it would only be until Gus hired someone to replace Mama. You already have a permanent job."

"Papa, we've talked about this," Jessie said, feeling weary. "You know how much I want to start my own business."

"If you stay at the cantina, it will be your business one day."

"How can I take over if you won't even let me in the kitchen? I can cook, Papa, you realize that, right?"

"You're better with the customers and the waitstaff than I am," her father said. "I like having you as the manager."

"You mean you like keeping everything exactly the way it is right now. You don't want to try anything new," Jessie corrected him.

"Let the girl pursue her own dream," Rosa-Maria said, interrupting them. "You're still a young man, Jose, and you have many years left to run the restaurant. Jessica doesn't want to wait another twenty years to realize her dream."

"I thought our dreams were the same—for her to take over the cantina!"

"Jose, you'll upset your mother." Gina gave her husband a warning look. "Can we talk about this another time?"

"*Abuela*, do you want me to come back to the house with you?" Jessie sought to change the subject. "We could watch a movie together, or maybe play cards."

"Thank you, Jessica, you're such a good girl," Rosa-Maria said. "I think I will rest. Come see me in a few days."

They had arrived at her father's car and Jessie bent to kiss her grandmother's cheek. "Please consider the cabin, okay? I think Gus misses you."

To her surprise, Rosa-Maria made a harrumphing sound. "He knows where to find me."

Jessie straightened and watched as her grandmother climbed into the car, and her parents loaded her flowers, balloons, and assorted belongings into the back of the SUV. Jessie was more certain than ever that something personal had happened between her grandmother and Gus. As far as she knew, Gus had not returned to the hospital after that first day, and aside from politely asking after Rosa-Maria each morning, he hadn't mentioned her. That, more than anything else, told Jessie something was wrong between the older couple.

After the SUV had left, Jessie brought the wheelchair back to the hospital lobby and returned to her own car. She drove into town where she dropped off three bags of laundry and retrieved three neatly washed, ironed, and folded bundles of freshly laundered items from the local dry cleaning and laundry service. Two bundles belonged to Gus and Evan and the third bundle contained sheets, towels, and other odds and ends. The cost was more than she had expected, but Gus paid her well. She placed the bundles into the laundry basket she'd brought with her and nearly collided with someone as she backed out of the door and onto the sidewalk.

"Oh, pardon me!" she exclaimed and then gasped as she looked up at the man holding the door. "Holt?"

"Jessica." His face registered pleasure and surprise, and something else that looked suspiciously like hunger, before he swiftly schooled his expression.

She'd seen very little of Holt in the past week and only from a distance. He'd been avoiding her, waiting until she'd left the kitchen before he made an appearance at any meal. By the time she returned to clear the dishes, he'd usually disappeared. Even Evan had commented on it, since Holt apparently also had a thing for sweets, but he'd skipped dessert every night since the incident with the ice cream. She knew it had to do with the kiss. He probably regretted it. But Jessie had been unable to forget it. The only thing she regretted was not letting the kiss lead to something more.

Now, seeing him look at her laundry basket, she raised her chin. She'd done nothing wrong, but she felt as if she'd just been caught in a fib. Then her eyes fell on the laundry bag Holt carried in one hand.

"I see I'm not the only one doing laundry today." She couldn't help but tease him, just a bit. "Your bunny slippers need cleaning?"

"Ha. No bunny slippers, just the usual guy stuff."

Glancing around as if afraid of being overheard, Jessie lowered her voice to a conspiratorial whisper. "You know this falls into the category of weird bachelor habits, right? You have a washing machine at home. What kind of man brings his *underwear* to the cleaners?"

Leaning forward, Holt put his mouth near her ear and whispered, "The kind that doesn't like when they turn pink in the wash."

Jessie smothered a surprised laugh. "Yes, I can't see that being a good look on you."

"This is easier, not to mention safer." He was smiling now and Jessie felt a warm glow that had nothing to do with the bright sunshine. "And I never lose any socks."

"Well, there's no sense in both of us bringing laundry into town. Next time just leave it with me and I'll bring it in."

"Or you could give me the basket each week and I'll take care of it," he countered. "There's no need for you to do the laundry, anyway."

"I don't mind. Although I admit I'm better at cooking than I am at housekeeping."

"You're exceptional at cooking." He patted his flat stomach. "If I don't watch it, I'm going to need to let my belt out another notch."

Jessie swallowed hard, remembering the firm, toned muscle that lay hidden beneath his clothing. She dragged her gaze upward. She spoke impulsively, the words escaping her mouth in a breathless rush before she could stop them. "You look good to me."

Suddenly, the air between them seemed overheated, charged with something electric and bright. Jessie couldn't see Holt's eyes behind his sunglasses, but she could feel his gaze on her like a palpable touch.

"I'm sorry," she blurted. "I shouldn't have said that."

"It's fine. Never apologize for honesty." Holt touched the brim of his hat. "Have a good day, ma'am."

He turned to enter the laundromat and Jessie briefly closed her eyes. He'd called her *ma'am*, a surefire sign she'd offended him, or at least made him uncomfortable to the point where he'd gone politely formal on her.

You look good to me.

Jessie mentally cringed. What had she been thinking? Of all the stupid things to say. Worse, she'd embarrassed Holt too. A sudden thought occurred to her and she quickly stepped in front of Holt, preventing him from entering the small shop. "About the laundry . . ."

She couldn't be sure, but she thought she detected a hint of humor in the curve of his lips. "What about it?"

"I'm sure he wouldn't care, but you won't tell Gus, will you?"

"Tell him what?"

She silently indicated the basket in her arms.

"It will be our secret," he replied.

Another secret.

"Thanks. I appreciate that."

"So, we're good?"

"I don't know," Jessie replied. "Are we?"

He tipped his head. "I'm not sure I take your meaning."

"Well," she began cautiously, knowing she was treading on dangerous—*personal*—ground, "it seems as if you might be avoiding me. I can't help but notice that whenever I prepare a meal, you don't come to the table with the others, but wait until after I've left the kitchen."

To her astonishment, two spots of ruddy color appeared high on his cheekbones. "I hadn't realized," he muttered. "It's purely coincidental."

"So you're not avoiding me?"

"Not at all."

For a man who seemed to value honesty, Jessie suspected he wasn't telling the truth. He had been avoiding her. The question was why?

"Okay, I'm glad to hear it." Jessie hesitated. "Since you're *not* avoiding me, do you—would you like to get a cup of coffee with me?"

She sensed both his surprise and his indecision.

"It's just coffee, Holt, not a lifetime commitment," she said wryly. "But, you're probably busy. It's just that I'd like to talk to you about something, if you have time."

He hesitated, and then nodded. "Sure. Let me drop this laundry off first."

Jessie indicated her own basket. "I'll just put this in the back of my Jeep."

She was parked nearby and, by the time she stowed the laundry basket and returned to the sidewalk, Holt was waiting for her, leaning indolently against one of the wooden posts that supported the covered walkway. He smiled at her as she approached and, for just an instant, Jessie allowed herself to imagine that he was hers, happy to see her.

"Where would you like to go? We could get coffee at Java Time, or coffee and something sweet at Kolaches."

She could tell by the hopeful note in his voice that he had a preference.

"Oh, I would love a piece of streusel cake," Jessie replied.

"Kolaches, it is."

The German bakery and breakfast restaurant and one of the more popular eateries in Last Stand. As they walked through the doors, Jessie saw this afternoon was no different. Most of the tables were occupied, but Holt located a booth for them near the large front windows, with a view over Main Street and the covered sidewalk. Jessie recognized many of the people inside the restaurant and was aware of the curious eyes that followed them. Most of the town was familiar with the Claiborne family dynamics and Jessie had once heard Holt described as one of Last Stand's most eligible—but unavailable—bachelors. Seeing them together like this would definitely cause some gossip. But if Holt was aware of the attention they drew, he gave no indication.

After removing his hat, he smoothed his hair with a quick slide of his fingers and then eased himself into the booth. Jessie slid in across from him, admiring his hands as he picked up the menu and perused it. They were the strong, capable hands of a man accustomed to hard work, but he kept them neat and clean. She remembered again how gentle those hands had been as he'd dressed her injured foot. He'd rolled his sleeves up over his forearms and beneath the light dusting of hair, his muscles flexed as he turned the pages of the menu.

"What looks good to you?"

"I think I'm also going to go with the streusel cake." He set the menu aside and leaned back. "It's always been my favorite."

"Mine too."

"So, what did you want to talk about?"

Jessie was prevented from replying when the waitress appeared.

"Two coffees and two streusel cakes, please," Holt said.

"We only have one serving of the streusel cake left," the waitress said. "It always sells out quick. Is there something else I can bring you instead?"

"I can order something else," Jessie said quickly, reaching for the menu.

"No, you have the streusel cake," Holt said, and reached for the menu at the same time. Their hands brushed briefly and Holt pulled back as if he'd been burned.

"We could share," Jessie offered, pushing her own hand down onto her lap. "I'm actually not that hungry."

"Are you sure?" When she nodded, he looked at the waitress. "One streusel cake, two forks."

After the waitress left, there was an awkward silence. Being around Holt always made her nervous and now she fought the urge to fidget beneath his steady regard. "Anyway," she said, gathering her courage, "I wanted to talk to you about my *abuela*."

"Is she okay? I visited her yesterday and she said she was going home today."

"Yes, she was actually released about an hour ago. She's staying with my parents until she decides what she wants to do next."

"But she's feeling good?"

"She seems a little tired, but otherwise she's doing great."

"I'm glad to hear it."

Leaning forward, Jessie lowered her voice so that only Holt could hear her. "Holt, do you think my grandmother and your father were . . . romantically involved?"

Holt's eyes widened slightly. "What makes you ask?"

Briefly, she described the scene she had witnessed at the hospital. "They seemed very much like a couple in love, but something must have happened because Gus didn't return to the hospital again to see her, and she acts very huffy whenever his name comes up."

Holt's expression had been neutral as she'd described the bedside scene. If the news surprised him, he hid it well.

"They've always been close," Holt said carefully. "But I've never seen anything to indicate their relationship went beyond that of employer and employee, or good friends."

"But you've had your suspicions," Jessie said triumphantly. "I can see it on your face."

"Maybe. I don't know."

"They've lived under the same roof for almost twenty-five years," Jessie persisted. "They probably know each other better than many married couples. In some ways, it almost seems natural for them to take their relationship to the next level, don't you think?"

"As in sleep together?"

"Why not? My grandmother is only sixty-three. She's still a vibrant, beautiful woman. Your father is what—sixty-five? He's attractive, in good health. Why shouldn't they have a romantic relationship? Realistically, they could be together for another twenty or thirty years."

"I don't know." Holt shook his head doubtfully. "My father is gun-shy. I can't see him putting himself out there again for any woman. He's been hurt too many times before."

"I understand, but his last divorce was years ago. Surely, he must get lonely."

"I'm sure he does, but he sees Rosa-Maria every day. She takes good care of him." His lips twisted in a wry smile. "They're practically married now. They live together but just don't have sex."

Jessie couldn't help but wonder if Holt was describing his own brief marriage. She was consumed with curiosity about what had happened ten years ago, but she would never dare ask. Holt and his father were alike in so many ways. Did Holt also get lonely? She knew he went out of town frequently on cattle business. Did he have women that he hooked up with when he traveled to Fort Worth and Houston? She hated even thinking about the possibility.

"They lived together," she corrected him. "And they haven't seen each other in days. My grandmother said if Gus wants to see her, he knows where to find her. She won't return to Riverrun Ranch. Besides, how do you know they weren't having sex?"

Holt made a scoffing sound. "I would know."

"Really?" Jessie propped her chin on her hand and considered him. "How?"

He gave her a tolerant look. "We all lived under the same roof. If something was going on between them, I would have known."

"Hmm. Doubtful. I'm sure he would have visited her in her apartment, which is on the other side of the house. He could have waited until you and Evan went to bed and then slipped down to see her. You're out at the barn before dawn; he could easily return to his own room later and you'd never know anything was going on."

Holt's eyes focused on her with a strange intensity, and Jessie could almost read his thoughts. He was thinking about their shared kiss and how easy it would have been to take it even further, in the privacy of the apartment. Would he ever dare pay her a midnight visit? The thought caused a delicious shiver to run through her body.

"You have this all figured out, don't you?" Holt leaned toward her and lowered his voice. "Okay, I'll admit that I've seen things over the past few years that have made me wonder."

Jessie leaned forward until their faces were close. She could see the texture of his skin, and the individual stubble on his jaw. Fixated on his mouth, she recalled again the sweet, hot tenderness of his kiss. "What kinds of things?"

"Looks, mostly. I've seen the way they look at each other when they think the other isn't aware. And when Rosa-Maria had her heart attack, I thought my father was going to collapse himself. He was terrified of losing her."

"Because he is *in love with her*. So why won't he see her, now that she's recovering?"

"I don't know." Holt shrugged and sat back in his chair. "He hasn't said anything to me."

"Maybe you could speak with him," Jessie suggested.

Holt raised his hands and laughed softly. "No. Definitely no."

"Why not?" A troubling thought occurred to Jessie. "Do you think my grandmother isn't good enough for your father?"

"What? Of course not!" The surprise in his voice was genuine. "I love Rosa-Maria, you know that. She's the best thing that ever happened to Riverrun Ranch, and probably the best thing that's ever happened to my father. But they're adults, Jessica. We should just let them work it out. I'm sure they wouldn't thank us for butting in."

"But my grandmother seems so unhappy," she pressed.

"If it's meant to be, they'll figure it out."

His tone was firm, and clearly, he didn't want to talk about his father and Rosa-Maria. Jessie knew he was probably right, but she loved her grandmother and only wanted her happiness.

The waitress returned with their coffee and a plate of streusel cake. They both reached for the two forks that rested on the plate and their hands collided again. This time, Holt didn't pull back but, instead, handed one fork to Jessie.

"You first," he said, holding her gaze. "I'll try to restrain myself and let you have your fair share."

Jessie laughed. "Oh, you have no idea who you're competing with, do you?"

"If you're trying to convince me you're a glutton, you'll have to do better than that," he said, indicating her neat forkful of streusel. "Watch and learn."

He took a hefty forkful for himself and his eyes closed briefly as he chewed. Jessie paused with her fork halfway to her mouth and stared, feeling a bit like a voyeur.

"Oh, yeah, that's good," he said, opening his eyes and smiling at her.

Jessie returned his smile, enjoying this lighter side of Holt that she so rarely saw.

"What other desserts do you like?" she asked, hoping she wasn't being too transparent. If the way to a man's heart really was through his stomach, she was going to make sure his taste buds were very happy.

"Peach cobbler is my favorite," he said. "Pecan pie is a close second, and I also like red velvet cake, but only if it's slathered in cream cheese frosting."

"I like peach cobbler, too, but I've never been a fan of red velvet. Give me a dark chocolate cake any day."

Holt took another bite of streusel. "I only eat chocolate in combination with caramel."

A shadow fell across their table and Holt abruptly stood, his face creasing into a smile. Jessie looked up to see Minna Herdmann and her granddaughter, Lynn. Minna was the unofficial matriarch of Last Stand, and her family had lived in town since before the incident with the Mexican army that had given the town its name. More than one hundred years old, she was someone everyone knew and respected. She was a tiny, wiry woman with long gray hair that she wore in a braid, wrapped neatly around her head, and despite her advanced years, her eyes were bright with curiosity. There was little that escaped her notice.

"Miss Minna." Holt reached out to take her hand, clasping it warmly between his two larger ones. "This is a pleasant surprise."

Minna beamed up at him like a young girl. "I could say the same, Holt Claiborne. I don't see you much these days and never in such pretty company." Her shrewd gaze turned to Jessie. "And Jessica, it's nice to see you out enjoying yourself. How is your grandmother doing?"

"She's out of the hospital and feeling much better," Jessie said. "Thank you so much for asking."

"I'm glad to hear it." Minna's gaze turned warm as her gaze moved between Jessie and Holt. "Life is short, even from my perspective. I heard she plans to retire, so my hope for her is that she can pursue whatever dreams she's put on hold, thinking she had time. The truth is, happiness doesn't wait for anyone. You need to grab it with both hands when it knocks on your door." She emphasized her words with a soft thrust of a gnarled fist before she leaned in toward Jessie. "And don't wait for a heart attack to wake you up."

"Yes, ma'am," Jessie said.

They watched as Lynn took the older woman's arm and led her toward a table near the back of the restaurant. Holt sat down again, but Jessie thought his expression looked troubled.

"She's an amazing woman," she ventured. "I can't believe she's over one hundred years old, and yet she somehow knows everything that goes on in this town."

Holt made a sound of agreement and took another bite of the streusel, but Jessie was willing to bet he no longer tasted the sweet dessert.

"Are you all right?"

Holt raised his gaze to hers. "Sure. Why do you ask?"

"Minna's advice about happiness . . . do you agree with her? About grabbing happiness when you can?"

Holt pushed the plate of streusel away and sat back in his chair. "What if there is no second chance at happiness, no next time? What if all you get is one shot at it and if you blow it, you're done?"

Jessie stared at him, more than a little taken aback by his response. Could he possibly believe happiness was not an option for himself?

"Sometimes," she said carefully, "you need a second chance, because you weren't quite ready for the first one. But if you *are* lucky enough to get a second chance at happiness, I believe you shouldn't waste it."

Holt's lips twisted. "I wish I could be as optimistic as you are."

Jessie didn't respond. Instead, she pulled the plate of streusel closer and took a generous forkful. Minna was right. Life was short and her own time with Holt was running out.

Chapter Nine

THUNDER ROLLED OVERHEAD, deep and rumbling. Standing on the terrace, Holt watched as lightning briefly illuminated the night sky. A breeze had kicked up, stirring the branches in the live oaks and cypress that surrounded the house. The storm would be on them soon. In between lightning strikes, the night was unrelentingly black.

"We're in for a doozy," observed Evan, who stood beside him with a beer in one hand. "You were right about moving the herds up to the high pasture this morning."

"They should be fine," Holt assured him. The high pastures had several three-sided shelters and they'd installed lightning rods, which would draw any strikes safely away from the cattle. "This will move through and blow over tonight."

Another crack of thunder split the air, and Evan jumped. "Damn, but that sounded like it was on top of us."

"I'm going to check on the momma cows," Holt said. "I don't need them getting spooked and injuring themselves."

"Do you want me to come with you?"

Hearing the reluctance in Evan's voice, Holt grinned. Evan hated thunderstorms. At least he no longer hid in his closet as he'd done when he was a child, but Holt wouldn't ask him to come down to the barns, not when there was a good likelihood they could be caught in a deluge. Even Sam had disappeared, as he usually did when a storm came up.

"No, I've got it covered."

"Excellent. I'll go through the house and close up the windows," Evan offered.

Three days had passed since Holt and Jessie had grabbed coffee together in town. Tonight was her night off, but she'd left all the fixings for grilled burgers, as well as a batch of homemade potato salad and chocolate moon pies with a thick, creamy filling for dessert. Holt had thrown the burgers onto the grill for himself, Evan, and Gus, but realized he hadn't seen Jessie since lunch. He didn't know if she was still on the ranch, or if she'd gone out for the evening.

As reluctant as he was to admit it, even to himself, they had turned a corner in their relationship since they'd had coffee together in town. He no longer avoided her at mealtimes, and she seemed less nervous when he was around. He looked forward to seeing her throughout the day and realized he'd missed her at dinner that night. He wished he knew where she was at the moment.

"Have you seen Jessie?"

Evan shook his head. "Nope. The last time I saw her was this afternoon. She was heading out to visit Rosa-Maria. Do you want me to check and see if she's returned?"

Holt told himself he wasn't worried about her. She was a grown woman, as Emmaline had pointed out. Besides, he didn't need to give Evan the wrong idea about himself and

Jessie. "No, thanks. I think she knows the generator will kick in if this thing knocks out the power."

Another deafening crack of thunder caused them both to look upward. "Yep, that's my cue to go check the windows," Evan said. "Good luck, bro."

Grabbing a flashlight, Holt made his away across the long expanse of lawn toward the barns. The air felt heavy and carried a coppery smell, a sure indication they were in for a fierce storm. At the entrance to the breeding barn, he slid one of the doors open and snapped on the overhead lights. The cows moved restlessly and Holt heard their deep, low bellows. They knew a storm was brewing too.

He passed the haymow on his left, where they kept several days' supply of hay and straw. There was a much larger hayloft on the upper level of the barn, but they generally kept several dozen bales on the main floor to feed the cows and line the pens. In the pens themselves, the animals had crowded into a corner, bumping against one another as they sought to escape the booming thunder. Holt grabbed several armfuls of fresh hay from the haymow and tossed them into each pen, hoping the distraction of fresh, sweet grass would help temper their nervousness. Another crack of thunder sounded, causing the cows to startle and scatter to the opposite corner of the pens.

Overhead, the lights flickered ominously.

"Damn it," Holt muttered. He turned to leave just as a flash outside the barn doors was followed almost immediately by another stunning clap of thunder, and the barn was plunged into darkness. Holt could smell the electrical discharge and knew the strike had been close. As he debated making a run for the house, the skies suddenly opened up and released a torrent of water, sheeting down in such copious amounts that it immediately churned the dirt into a river of mud in front of the barn.

Another flash lit up the yard and Holt muttered a curse. In that brief instant of brilliance, a figure ran through the rain near the paddock, ducking low as the lightning lashed across the sky.

Jessica.

Fears, pure and hot and primal, drove Holt outside and across the yard. The downpour was so intense, he could barely see. Water gushed off the brim of his hat, instantly soaked his shirt and pants, and swirled around his feet, creating a thick mud that sucked at his boots.

He ran into Jessica halfway across the yard, her head down as she bolted toward the barn.

"Holt!" she cried when she saw him. "What are you doing out here?"

"Rescuing you!" He had to shout to be heard over the thundering rain.

He wasn't sure, but he thought she grinned at him through the deluge, before she caught his hand and pulled him toward the structure. Another bolt of lightning rent the air, not as close as before but close enough that Holt bent protectively over Jessie's slighter form. The accompanying crack of thunder was a heartbeat behind, and then they were safely inside the barn. Jessica leaned forward, hands on her knees, pulling in deep breaths.

"Are you okay?" Holt removed his dripping hat and swiped the rain from his face.

She nodded, not looking up. "Yeah, thanks."

"Don't move, I'll grab a lantern."

They kept several battery-operated lanterns on hooks inside the door for just this reason, and Holt quickly retrieved two and turned them on. He set one on a nearby worktable and hung the second from a hook on one of the barn's enormous support posts. Even in the soft, intimate glow he could see Jessie wore a sleeveless summer dress that was now plastered against her skin. Her dark hair was slicked back from her face and hung in damp ropes around her shoulders, and her bare arms gleamed wetly.

"Where are your shoes?" he demanded, seeing her bare feet.

She straightened and waved a hand toward the yard where the rain continued to beat down. "Somewhere out there. They came off in the mud."

As if to punctuate her words, lightning flashed again and thunder rolled overhead. Jessie flinched, and Holt saw she was shaking. The air temperature had dropped with the incoming storm and Holt became aware that his own clothing was uncomfortably wet and heavy.

"You're chilled," he said. "Hang on."

Taking one of the lanterns, he made his way to the supply room and took down two of the heavy wool bedding blankets and several clean towels they used for calving.

"Here, let's get you dry." He used one of the towels to briskly rub her arms. Up close, her eyelashes were spiky with moisture, and water traced tiny rivulets down her smooth neck. "I'd suggest we make a run for the house, but it's too dangerous."

"I've seen thunderstorms before," Jessie said, "but never like this. I actually thought I was going to be killed."

Holt paused in his ministrations. "What were you doing out there?"

"I almost always go for a walk on the property after dinner is cleared away. I had a phone call from my mother, so I got a late start tonight. I thought I'd be back to the house before dark, and definitely before the rain started, but this storm just rolled in so fast." She searched his eyes. "What are you doing out here?"

"Checking on the cows. Thunder spooks them."

"Storms are scary, but I love them," Jessie said. "They're exhilarating."

Holt understood. He felt the same way during storms. He felt that way now, alone with Jessica.

Energized.

A little in awe.

Desperate to kiss her again and hopeful about his future in a way he hadn't been in a very long time. Rain drummed against the roof of the barn and came down in sheets outside the door but inside, they were cocooned in soft light and warmth, surrounded by the fragrant smell of sweet hay and oats. Jessie was looking at him in a way he found difficult to refuse and suddenly he didn't want to. He let his gaze travel over her face, taking in the wide, dark eyes, the curve of her cheeks and her full, soft lips. The towel dropped from his fingers.

He cupped her face in his hands, his thumbs stroking over her damp cheeks. Lowering his head, he covered her mouth with his own. Jessie's lips parted softly against his and she slid one hand to the back of his neck, drawing him closer. The kiss was as lush and sweet as a summer peach. When Holt finally lifted his head, his heart was beating hard. Jessie opened her eyes and he could see they were a little hazy with pleasure. He wanted to drag her back into his arms and kiss her until she no longer knew or cared that they were in a cow barn in the middle of a thunderstorm. He wrapped his arms around her to draw her into an embrace, but their clothes were soggy and cold, causing them to step quickly apart with startled laughter.

"Oh, you're soaking wet!" Jessie exclaimed. "I'm so sorry—that's not good!"

"We're both drenched," Holt agreed. "Here, wrap this around yourself." Shaking out the wool blanket, he draped it around her shoulders. "Better?"

"Yes, but what about you?" She slanted him an endearingly suggestive smile. "You should probably take your shirt off before you catch cold."

Holt arched one eyebrow, but began unbuttoning his shirt. "Why am I not convinced it's my health you're interested in?"

He peeled the sopping shirt off and wrung it out before hanging it on a hook, acutely aware of Jessie's fascinated attention. He kept himself in shape, but he couldn't recall the last time he'd been this self-conscious in front of a woman. As he reached for the second blanket, Jessie put a hand on his arm.

He stilled and then turned.

"What I'm really interested in," she said, sounding cautious, "is another kiss like the one you just gave me."

"Jessica," he warned softly, even as his heart leaped in anticipation. "This is a bad idea."

"I won't tell anyone," she promised. "It will be another one of our secrets."

She put her hands on his bare chest and Holt was a goner. He felt the shock of her touch all the way to the soles of his boots. She trailed her fingers across his collarbones and down the shallow groove that bisected his pecs. Holt didn't dare move in case she came to her senses and stopped. His breathing grew shallow and his stomach muscles contracted when her fingertips traced their way down to his belt buckle and stopped. Hooking her fingers around the belt, she took two steps back to where he'd stacked the hay bales, tugging him with her.

Holt didn't resist.

She kissed him, her mouth fusing softly with his. Her lips were warm and velvety and she tasted of sweet tea and lemons. Holt angled his head, seeking more contact and was rewarded when he felt the sleek slide of her tongue against his. Groaning his approval, he gathered her against his body. The wool blanket slid from her shoulders and onto the floor, and through the damp warmth of her dress, he could feel her supple curves.

He wanted to consume her. He wanted to lay her down

on the hay bales and peel her dress off. He wanted to use his hands and mouth to worship all the smooth, golden skin that he'd only fantasized about. He ran his hands over the rounded curve of her hips and filled his palms with her perfect derrière. Jessie speared her fingers through his hair, deepening the kiss. Holt's body had gone hard the moment he felt her tongue pushing against his. He'd been celibate for too long because the feel and taste of her caused every cell in body to stand up and take notice. He was painfully aroused.

Breaking the kiss, he bent her over his arm and dragged his mouth along the side of her neck, pausing at the hollow of her throat to press his lips against the spot where her pulse visibly throbbed. She clutched his bare shoulders and her breath came in warm pants against his cheek.

"May I see you?" He *needed* to see her. He'd never wanted anything more in his life.

Her dress had slender straps and it took only a flick of his fingers to push one over her shoulder and down her arm, freeing her breast. Her breath hitched as cool air wafted over her bare skin and caused her nipple to tighten. Holt nearly groaned out loud at the sight. He covered her with his hand and gently cupped the round, firm flesh.

"You're so damned pretty," he said with heartfelt sincerity. Cupping her breast, he bent his head and drew the dusky tip into his mouth. Jessie made a soft gasping sound and arched upward. Holt swirled his tongue around her nipple before drawing sharply on it, and then rolled the sensitized nub gently between his fingers, watching as Jessie's eyes drifted closed and her mouth parted on a soft *oh* of pleasure.

He kissed the side of her throat, inhaling her fragrance, before nibbling his way to the tender spot beneath her ear.

"I want you to touch me."

"I am touching you." He smiled against her soft skin.

"No. I want you to touch me . . . here." Taking his hand, she brought it down to the apex of her thighs.

Holt swallowed hard, feeling both moved and excruciatingly aroused by her boldness and her trust. Dragging the hem of her dress up, he flattened his hand over the satiny skin of her stomach and then slid his fingers beneath the scrap of silk she wore. She widened her stance as he dipped lower and explored her soft, wet folds. He fastened his mouth over hers, tangling his tongue with hers as he parted her and pushed one finger into her welcoming tightness. She made a deep groaning sound of pleasure as Holt slowly stroked his finger in and out and used his thumb to torment the tiny rise of sensitized flesh. Jessie clung to him and her hips strained against his hand. Suddenly, it became important to him that she reach climax. He wanted to see her come apart in his arms and watch her expression as he brought her to the peak of pleasure.

"Come for me," he breathed against her mouth. His words seemed to enflame her. Outside, the rain drummed down on the ground but he was so absorbed in Jessie's response, he barely noticed. Her body flooded his fingers with slick moisture. She was intensely aroused and the knowledge filled Holt with supreme satisfaction. *He* had done this. *He* had aroused her.

She closed her eyes. Her breathing was rapid and uneven,

and her fingers dug into the muscles of his arms. Holt knew the precise instant when her orgasm hit her. She clutched at him and cried out, even as her entire body tightened and shuddered. Holt kissed her, spearing his tongue into her mouth and absorbing her soft cries. He'd never experienced anything so erotic and he didn't stop stroking her until he'd wrung every last shiver from her, and she finally went limp and pliant against him. Lifting his head, he carefully adjusted her clothing, drew her down onto the hay bale bench, and gathered her into the curve of his body. She laughed softly and turned her face against his shoulder.

"I can't believe we just did that." Her voice was muffled but Holt heard the blush in her voice. "I've never done anything like this, really."

He tightened his arm around her and when she lifted her face, he bent and covered her mouth with his own. The kiss was soft and sumptuous, her lips generous and yielding beneath his. She caressed the bare skin of his chest and stomach with one hand, but when her fingers moved to the buckle of his belt, he covered her hand with his.

"Jessica—"

"Let me." She searched his eyes in the muted light. "Let me do for you what you just did for me."

"You don't have to do anything for me," he said, but behind the zipper, he was rigid with arousal.

"But what if I want to? Holt—" But whatever else she might have said was lost as the figure of a man appeared in the open doorway of the barn.

"Holt! Are you here?" Evan called.

In his entire life, Holt had never felt the urge to hurt his brother, but right now, he could have cheerfully choked the younger man. But he also acknowledged his timing couldn't have been better. He'd saved Holt from doing something he'd probably regret tomorrow. Recognizing what it must have cost Evan to come down to the barn in the middle of the storm, he drew in a deep, steadying breath.

"Over here," he replied, watching as Jessie wrapped the wool blanket around her shoulders and moved to the far side of the hay mow, away from him. Holt retrieved his wet shirt and pulled it on.

Evan came forward until he stood near the opening of the hay mow and his gaze flicked between the two of them. "So, you found Jess. When you didn't come back, I thought I should check that you didn't get swept away. It's like a river out there."

"Yeah, Jessica got caught in the worst of it. One of the strikes came down just outside the barn door." Holt retrieved his hat from the hook. "You didn't bring an umbrella by any chance, did you?"

Evan shook his head. "Nope. I'm not a fan of turning myself into a lightning rod. We'll have to make a run for it."

Holt turned to Jessie. "Think you can do that?"

She gave him a smile that was full of meaning. "Why not? After all, I'm already wet."

An image of her in his arms came rushing back—as if he would ever be able to forget the sight of her face in the throes of an orgasm. Holt dragged in a deep, steadying breath. He needed to get a grip, because he badly wanted to haul Jessica somewhere private and show her just how much he wanted her.

"You go ahead with Jessica," Evan said. "I'll close the barn doors."

They stood for a moment, looking at the driving rain. Holt could see a porch light on at the main house, which meant the generator had kicked on. Now he looked at Jessica's bare feet and the swirling river of red mud she would need to navigate before they reached the grassy lawn.

"Do you want me to carry you?"

"Definitely not. Let's go." Without waiting for him, she dashed into the storm, using one hand to protect her face as she ran toward the house. Holt helped Evan slide the big doors closed and secured them before they bolted after her.

Gus waited for them on the covered porch with an armful of towels.

"Best get into a warm shower before you catch a chill. The generator is working so you should have plenty of hot water."

"Great idea." Evan shook the water from his hat. "I could use a drink too."

"Come down to the study when you're dry," Gus said. "I have a good bottle of Cowboy Bourbon."

"Give me ten minutes," Evan replied, and disappeared into the house.

"Will you join us?" Gus included both Holt and Jessie in his invitation.

"Thank you, but I think I'm going to soak in a warm tub and then curl up in bed with a good book," Jessie said.

"Good night."

Before Holt could say anything to stop her, she fled into the house.

"Everything okay, son?"

"Yeah, I was checking the cows. They're fine."

"That's not what I meant."

Holt glanced at his father, then sighed. The old man was still as sharp as a tack and didn't miss much.

"I know." Holt walked to edge of the porch and braced his hands on the railing as he watched the rain. "Dad? Have you ever wanted something you had no right to want?"

"Every day, son." Gus came to stand beside him. "She's a lovely young woman and she obviously has feelings for you. How long have you been interested in her?"

"Am I that transparent?"

"Only to me and only because I know you so well."

Holt scrubbed his hands over his face and then looked at his father. "I worry that I'm not right for her, that she'll tire of me within a year. I'm the responsible one, remember?" He gave a huff of laughter. "When has that ever been exciting?"

"She strikes me as someone who appreciates the meaning of hard work and understands the importance of family. I believe her values are aligned closely with your own."

Holt angled his head to look at his father. "She doesn't know me. Not really."

"Well then, why don't you give her the chance?"

Holt blew out a hard breath and when he spoke, his voice was little more than a whisper. "What if I can't make it work? Having her, and then losing her—" He couldn't finish the sentence.

"You wonder if she'll be like Alyssa."

Holt looked away, unwilling to admit his fear.

"Fortune hunting is much like diving for treasure," Gus said drily. "Alyssa excelled at it. But do you really think Jessie is anything like your ex-wife?"

Holt thought about the woman he'd been married to for four years, realizing he hadn't really known her at all. He'd never guessed that the pretty girl he'd been so infatuated with had known more about his own balance statement than he did. He had been interested in stocks from the time he'd turned thirteen and had used his summer earnings to invest in the stock market, under his grandfather's watchful eye. He'd started with penny stocks and, by the time he turned twenty-one, he was worth more than two million dollars. Stupid young boy that he'd been, he'd believed Alyssa had loved him for himself.

"She was only ever interested in my portfolio."

Gus chuckled. "If she'd taken her job more seriously and done her homework a little better, she would have realized who your grandfather was and stuck around a few years longer. What she ended up with was a drop in the bucket compared to what you now have."

Holt hated to think what might have happened if he'd still been married to Alyssa when his grandfather died. Maybe she would have decided he was worth hanging on to. Maybe she would have tried to rob him of his inheritance. He'd never know, thank God.

"It's been ten years since your marriage ended, son. Alyssa was an unfortunate mistake. But don't lock your heart away because you're afraid of getting hurt again." Gus laughed softly. "Listen to me, talking like an old fool. I'm hardly the one to give you relationship advice, not with my track record."

Holt slanted his father a rueful grin. "Yeah, we're a pair."

"The difference is, you're still young. You could still have a lifetime of happiness with the right woman." Gus clapped him on the back. "Life is short, son. Don't spend it alone."

After his father had gone into the house, Holt stayed on the porch, listening to the distant storm and watching the rain come down. He thought about what his father had said and knew in his heart he was right. He'd always imagined himself with a wife and a bunch of kids, but after Alyssa, he'd never wanted to put himself out there again.

Until now.

Did he dare take a chance on Jessica? She could have any man she wanted. Why would she saddle herself with him, a guy who admittedly had commitment issues? Even if he did allow himself to begin a relationship with her, there was no guarantee he could live up to her expectations or make her happy for the long haul. His own experience aside, statistics were against most marriages working, as evidenced by his own father's track record. Not that he was ready to pro-pose—he'd made a promise to himself never to marry again. But he wouldn't lie to himself, either; he wanted her more than he'd ever wanted another woman in his life. Even his ex-wife, Alyssa, hadn't aroused him the way Jessica did.

What could he do when she tempted him at every turn?

When he couldn't get her out of his head and there was no escaping her presence in his house and in his life? Hell, he couldn't even take her to bed because if things didn't work out, it could cause tension between their two families. But what if he could make it work? Did he have the courage to put his heart on the line again?

Chapter Ten

"**I** DON'T THINK I can continue working at the ranch."

Two days had passed since the incident in the barn and Holt had once again taken to avoiding mealtimes—and Jessie. She was done. She had no idea how to get close to him when their relationship was always one step forward and two steps back. Now she and Jorie were at Java Time, the downtown coffee shop where they met every Saturday morning for coffee and girl talk. But Jessie couldn't bring herself to tell Jorie about her encounter with Holt in the barn. It felt too intimate and too personal, and she didn't fully understand her own feelings about what had happened. She only knew she couldn't get him out of her head.

Every time she remembered her own boldness, she cringed. She'd done exactly what she'd told herself she would never do to Holt—she'd taken the lead and had practically begged him to have sex with her. It was beyond mortifying, especially considering she'd been so turned on and yet he hadn't allowed her to reciprocate. That, more than anything, was what continued to haunt her. Why would he give her an amazing orgasm, but refuse to let her do the same for him? She wanted to die every time she thought about it.

"What will you do?"

Jessie shrugged. "I can go back to the restaurant and continue working until I have enough money saved for the food truck, or I can take out a loan and just do it."

"Seems like a simple decision, Jess. You don't want to stay at the ranch and you don't want to go back to the cantina. So go buy your truck and get on with your dream."

"And leave Riverrun, which means I'll never see Holt." Jessie made a groaning sound of frustration and scrubbed her hands over her face. "I'm so confused. I know Holt is attracted to me, but he's too gun-shy to follow his instincts."

Jorie sipped her coffee. "You can't blame the guy for being cautious. From what Luke told me, his ex really did a number on him."

"But it's been almost ten years! He deserves to be happy."

"I totally agree. Maybe you just need to be a little more upfront about what you want. Actually talk to him about it." Jorie looked at her watch. "Sorry, but I have to get over to the shelter. Aren't you working today?"

Jessie shrugged. "Gus and Evan are driving up to Fort Worth today to look at some cattle and won't return until tomorrow. Gus said Holt will take care of his own lunch and dinner, so the day is mine. I have some errands to run in town, I'll go over and visit my grandmother, and then maybe I'll stop by the bank and talk to someone about that loan."

"Sounds perfect," Jorie said. "Good luck and let me know how it goes."

Jessie left the coffee shop and stopped at her car to retrieve a laundry basket before she made her way along Main

Street to the cleaners to pick up the laundry she'd dropped off earlier in the week. She paid for the three bundles of clean laundry and was just turning away when the girl behind the counter stopped her.

"You're picking up for the Claiborne family, right?"

Jessie nodded. "Right."

"Hang on, I have one more bundle." She disappeared to the back of the shop and returned with a neatly folded and wrapped stack of clothing. "Here you go."

The clothing belonged to Holt and seeing the bundle made her think about the day they had shared the streusel. She had been so certain then that their relationship was moving in the right direction, and that by the time her four weeks were up, they would be on their way toward having a real one.

"Thanks," she said and accepted the clothing.

She drove out to her parents' house, a cute one-story home situated under a canopy of pecan trees.

"Hello?" she called as she opened the door.

"In here, honey!" Her mother came out of the kitchen. "What a nice surprise. I wasn't expecting to see you today."

"I unexpectedly have the day off, so I thought I'd come over to say hello." Jessie handed her mother a covered basket. "I made us something for lunch. Shrimp soft tacos with avocado cilantro and rhubarb salsa. Where's *abuela*?"

"She's on the back porch. Go sit with her, and I'll bring out some sweet tea."

Jessie found her grandmother shelling peas and humming lightly to herself. She looked up as Jessie approached and broke into a smile.

"Jessica, how lovely! Come sit with me, child."

Jessie sat down on the wicker sofa next to her grand-mother and watched her nimble fingers snap the pea pods. "How are you feeling?"

"Like a million bucks." Her dark eyes twinkled as if she had a secret. "How is everything at the ranch? The boys came to visit me several days ago and it sounds like you're settling in very well."

Jessie looked down at her hands. "Actually, I'm going to give Gus my notice. I can't even last four weeks, *abuela*."

Rosa-Maria stopped shelling the peas and turned to look at Jessie, her dark eyes shrewd. "You knew this might happen."

Jessie nodded, feeling unexpected tears threaten. "I did. But I didn't know it would be this hard. He runs hot and cold, kissing me one day and avoiding me the next."

She didn't have to say Holt's name. Her grandmother knew how she felt about him.

The older woman took one of Jessie's hands in her own. Her skin was warm and dry, but her grip was strong. "Four weeks isn't a very long time to win someone over, especially when that someone is a Claiborne." She gave Jessie a wry smile. "Trust me. I know. The Claiborne men are a proud, stubborn bunch. But I know those boys. I practically raised them. They went through so much as children. First Holt's poor mother died while he was an infant. Then the twins' mother left when Evan and Luke were just toddlers. Then Emmaline's mother left and went to New York, taking

Emmaline with her. Can you imagine how difficult that was for them? More so for Holt, because he was older. He loved both of his stepmothers and his sister, but his love wasn't enough to prevent them leaving. Then when his wife did what she did—well, it's no wonder he's reluctant to take any chances."

Jessie sniffed and wiped her eyes. "I know all of that and I get it, I really do. I just don't know how to convince him to take a chance on me. I've been crazy about him since I was about fifteen, but I don't think he sees me as a grown woman who knows what she wants."

"Do you love him?"

Jessie stared at her grandmother as she considered the question. "I don't know. I think so. All I can tell you is my heart starts to race every time he comes into the room. I can't sleep, I can't eat . . . I think about him all the time. He's smart and he's gentle and kind. I love making him smile and when he looks at me—" She broke off with an embarrassed laugh. "All I know is, I can't be in the same house with him if he's indifferent to me."

Her mother stepped onto the porch carrying a tray of sweet tea and a plate of cookies. She set it down on the table and took the chair across from Jessie. "I believe Holt Claiborne is anything but indifferent to you," she said.

"I agree," Rosa-Maria said. "When he was here the other day, he seemed very quiet. The only time he perked up was when your name came up in conversation."

"Maybe leaving the ranch is exactly what you need to do," her mother said, pouring each of them a glass of tea.

"Nothing piques a man's interest more than something he can't have. After all, look what it's done for your grandmother."

To Jessie's astonishment, Rosa-Maria's cheeks turned pink. "What do you mean?" She turned to look at the older woman. "Does this have something to do with Gus?"

"Why would you ask that?"

Jessie's gaze lingered on her grandmother, noting the sudden tension in her hands and back. "Because I saw him at the hospital with you, in your room. You looked . . . in love."

Rosa-Maria nodded and raised her gaze to Jessie's. "Yes. I have loved Gus Claiborne for more than twenty years."

Jessie leaned forward. "I saw him holding your hand, *abuela*. He looked at you like a man in love."

"He says he loves me. He wants me to return to the ranch, but I told him I would only go back as Mrs. Claiborne and not his housekeeper. He's been hurt too many times, so he doesn't trust me not to do the same thing to him." Her voice was firm. "But those were my conditions. I told him if he wants me in his life, he will marry me."

Jessie stared at her grandmother, too stunned to respond.

"He can't doubt her love for him," Gina said over the rim of her glass. "Rosa-Maria has stood by his side for nearly twenty-five years."

"Until now," Rosa-Maria murmured.

"No, no," Jessie protested, clutching her grandmother's hand. "You had a heart attack! That's hardly the same as abandoning him."

"What he doesn't know is that I'd return even if he chooses not to marry me," she said quietly. "Life is too short to turn your back on happiness. And Gus makes me happy."

Jessie was quiet for a moment, recalling Minna Herdmann's words at the German bakery.

Happiness doesn't wait for anyone. You need to grab it with both hands when it knocks on your door.

"So, what will you do if you leave the ranch?" Rosa-Maria changed the subject. "Will you finally start your food truck business?"

"That's my plan. I was actually going to stop by the bank this afternoon and talk to them about a loan. I don't have enough money saved yet, so unless I want to wait another year, I'll need to borrow the rest."

Her mother and grandmother exchanged a meaningful look.

"What?" Jessie demanded. "What was that look?"

"Do you want to tell her or shall I?" Rosa-Maria asked Gina.

"Your grandmother has been putting money away for you since the day you were born," Gina said.

Jessie's heart swelled with love for her grandmother, who had so little, but was so generous. "*Abuela*, that's incredibly sweet and generous, but I don't want you to give me any money. You need that for your retirement."

But Rosa-Maria held up one hand, forestalling any further protests. "I originally started saving money for your college education," she said. "But then you got the scholarship to culinary school and didn't need any assistance, so I decided it would be for your wedding. But maybe you'd like to use part of it for your food truck."

Jessie stared at the two women with growing unease. "How much money are we talking about?"

When her grandmother named a six-figure amount, Jessie's mouth fell open. "*Abuela!* That amount would pay for a college education, a wedding, *and* a food truck! How could you possibly have saved so much money?"

Rosa-Maria smiled in satisfaction. "I took investing advice from a very smart teenager, who grew into an extremely smart young man. Holt has been handling my money for me since he was fifteen years old."

"Holt has been investing your money for twenty years?" Jessie exclaimed. "How did I not know this?"

"It's been our secret," Rosa-Maria said. "But I did it for you and I want you to have it."

Jessie shook her head. "But it's too much. I only need a fraction of the amount to purchase the food truck. You need to keep the rest."

"I have enough funds to be very comfortable in retirement."

Jessie looked between the two women. "Does Papa know?"

Rosa-Maria shrugged. "He knows."

"This is too much to take in," Jessie protested. "I feel as if I'm in a dream."

"Your grandmother wants you to have the money," her mother urged her. "I know how important this food truck is to you and your father will come around, once he sees how happy you are. That's all he wants."

"I don't know." Jessie hesitated. "Let me think about it. I'd feel better if I could just borrow what I need to purchase the truck, with a promise to pay you back."

"There's no need to repay anything," Rosa-Maria assured her. "I'm just so happy that I can do this for my only grandchild."

Overwhelmed, Jessie hugged her grandmother and kissed her cheek. "Thank you, *abuela*. You have no idea what this means to me."

"Oh, I think I do." She laid a hand on Jessie's arm. "Let Holt know the amount you need; he manages the account and he'll take care of the details."

A thread of unease unwound itself in her stomach as Jessie thought about talking to Holt. He'd been so remote since the thunderstorm that she found herself hesitant to approach him about anything for fear of being rejected. But she wouldn't let her grandmother see any of that.

"Thank you, *abuela*," she said again. "I love you so much."

"No more than I love you, child."

Jessie returned to her car, feeling as if she was floating on air. She still couldn't believe her clever grandmother had managed to sock away so much money over the course of twenty years. That Holt had been instrumental in helping her to do that didn't surprise her. She'd known he was smart and he'd always looked after those he loved; she just hadn't known he was a financial wizard.

Instead of driving back to the ranch, Jessie stopped at the

grocery store and then made her way to her little cottage on the river. She hadn't spent much time there since she'd begun working at Riverrun Ranch. The view from her deck of the beautiful Pedernales River never failed to make her feel better about things. One way or the other, she'd find a way to be okay, with or without Holt Claiborne in her life.

After sorting through her mail, she unpacked the groceries and ran a load of laundry, all the while debating how she would break the news to Gus that she would be leaving Riverrun. True, she hadn't been there for very long, but Gus had maintained a cook and housekeeper for more than twenty-five years. She would give him two weeks' notice, but who would he hire after she left? Would her grandmother agree to return, as she'd said she would?

Happy to be in her own small kitchen, Jessie prepared a savory sausage-and-cheddar-cheese bread pudding for the following morning and then made a batch of oversized blueberry muffins with a sugary-crumb topping. The tradition of the men coming back to the house for breakfast after the early morning chores was a long one. Even if Gus and Evan didn't return the following morning, Luke and Cort sometimes came up to the main house to eat. She wanted to ensure there was plenty of food to keep the men satisfied.

Covering the bread pudding and the muffins, Jessie carried them out to the car. The ranch house was dark when she pulled into the driveway ten minutes later, but the lights were on in the cattle barns, indicating Holt and Cort were still working. She sat in the car for several minutes, unable to put a name to the ache in her chest.

She loved everything about Riverrun Ranch. She had so many wonderful childhood memories of days spent with either Emmaline or Callie, or just watching her grandmother prepare meals for the Claiborne family. She recalled when she had first begun to notice Holt as more than just her friend's older brother. He had returned to the ranch following his divorce and had moved back into the main house. At the time, he was only twenty-five years old and Jessie was sixteen, almost seventeen. She'd come to the ranch more often that next year in hopeful anticipation of seeing him. If he'd noticed her at all, it was simply to nod a greeting. But by the time she'd graduated from culinary school four years later, her crush on him was complete. He was ruggedly handsome, mysteriously stoic, and hardworking. Most of all, he understood the importance of family. For as long as Jessie could recall, he'd looked out for his siblings. He'd even tried to chase Cort off when he'd believed him to be a fortune hunter after Emmaline's money.

But only in her wildest dreams did Holt Claiborne hold her in his arms and touch her as intimately as he had in the barn. She'd always thought him sexy, but she'd never thought she would see him set aside his cool reserve as he had that night. He'd surprised her with his passion and his tender expertise. The man knew his way around a woman's body. Now that she'd experience him for herself, she craved more. She wanted to show him that she could please him, the way he had pleased her.

She wanted to show him that she was the perfect woman for him.

Sadly, she didn't know if she would have the opportunity, since he seemed determined to avoid her again, and soon, she'd leave Riverrun Ranch for good. She figured she only had a week—maybe two—to catch her cowboy.

Chapter Eleven

I T TOOK JESSIE two trips to bring the food and the laundry into the house. Sam was asleep on the back terrace and he came into the kitchen to greet her, his tail thumping happily against her legs.

"Hey, boy," she said, bending down to stroke his ears. "What are you doing up here? Don't you know Holt is down at the barn?" The yellow lab generally followed Holt everywhere so Jessie was surprised to see him at the house. "Is it time for your supper? Is that why you're up here?"

After putting the bread pudding into the fridge, she measured out some dry dog food and watched as Sam enthusiastically began to wolf it down. She brought the laundry basket upstairs and left Gus's and Evan's bundles on top of their dressers. She stored the sheets and towels in the linen closet and carried Holt's freshly laundered clothing to his room.

Jessie opened the door and stepped into the dark bedroom. She'd taken no more than four steps toward the bed when she realized she'd made a mistake. Light shone from under the adjoining bathroom door and she could hear someone—*Holt*—moving around. Jessie froze, but as she turned to creep out of the room, the bathroom door opened and Holt stood silhouetted in the doorway, wearing nothing but a pair of boxer briefs that hugged his strong thighs and emphasized his masculine assets.

Jessie gaped at him, unable to move or even formulate words to explain why she was standing in the middle of his bedroom. Steam wreathed around him as he stared at her. His hair was wet and his skin gleamed with moisture. The muscles that had made her go boneless in the barn were on full display, and the light from the bathroom cast intriguing shadows over the sculpted contours of his shoulders and arms. She saw again the light furring of chest hair that tapered down his stomach and disappeared beneath the elastic waistband of his boxers. Her fingers itched to follow that path.

"Jessica." She could hear the surprise in his deep voice. "What are you doing here?"

"I didn't know you were here," she said quickly. "I thought you were down at the barn." She held out the bundle of clothing. "I was picking up the laundry and they gave me yours. I was just—I was—"

Holt crossed the space that separated them and the bundle of clothing slipped from fingers that had suddenly gone nerveless. He stopped just inches from her and Jessie could feel the energy that radiated from him. The air vibrated with awareness. His blue eyes were intent on her face, and she made no protest when he reached out and lifted a strand of her hair from her shoulder and rubbed it between his fingers. He was so close that even in the indistinct light, she saw the water that trickled along the side of his neck.

"I've tried to stay away from you," he muttered, his voice low and rough. "God knows I've tried, but it's been hell, and now here you are, and I'll be damned if I let you go without doing this."

Jessie went still as he bracketed her face in his hands, his thumbs stroking lightly along her cheekbones. Then he bent his head and kissed her, cautiously at first, as if he expected her to protest. But the first touch of his mouth against hers snapped her out of the trance she'd been in. She kissed him back, parting her lips and inviting the touch of his tongue against hers. Holt grunted in assent and hauled her into his arms.

In the space of a heartbeat, everything changed.

Holt slanted his mouth hard over hers and deepened the kiss, sinking his tongue deep into her mouth until Jessie went weak with the pleasure of it. She clung to him, her hands pressed against the bare skin of his back. He was warm and solid and she could feel the flex of his muscles beneath her fingers. He tasted of minty toothpaste and smelled of something woodsy and citrusy.

She wanted to consume him.

Holt lifted his head and his blue eyes glittered hotly. "If you want to leave, you should go now. If you stay, I'm taking you to bed."

Jessie's heart, already racing, nearly stopped. As declarations went, it wasn't overly romantic, but it was enough for her. If she left now, she'd likely never have this chance again. He'd rebuke himself for his moment of weakness and ensure there was no repeat offer. If she left now, he'd take it as a personal rejection and the walls he kept so carefully erected would be raised even higher.

For half an instant, she couldn't breathe. Holt's eyes showed raw need and heat, just barely banked. He wasn't making her any promises, but she didn't care. Right now, she didn't want anything beyond this moment, this night. She'd leave the ranch in the morning, since she wouldn't work for Gus and carry on an affair under his roof. But Gus was gone tonight and there was no reason not to stay. Tomorrow, when she was no longer employed at Riverrun Ranch, she and Holt could talk about a future.

Their future.

"I'll stay," she said softly, and punctuated her words with a soft kiss, wreathing her arms around his neck. "Of course I'll stay. I *want* to stay."

Holt groaned and speared his fingers in her hair, angling her head for better access as he plundered her mouth again. Jessie sagged against him, allowing him to feast on her lips. His kiss was hot and urgent, and an answering heat unfurled and blossomed low in Jessie's midsection. She clutched his arms, curling her fingers around his hard biceps, because the room seemed to spin around them as he kissed her. She wasn't aware of anything except the moist warmth of his lips against hers. When he finally lifted his head and stepped away long enough to kick the bedroom door closed, she felt lost. Light from the bathroom spilled into the bedroom, illuminating him. His eyes were hungry as he turned back to her.

"I need to see you." His hands went to the hem of her T-shirt and he pulled it up and over her head. Without breaking eye contact, he reached behind her and deftly unfastened her bra, then let it slide free of her arms and drop to the floor beside her shirt. His gaze dropped to her breasts and he dragged in an unsteady breath. "You're the most beautiful woman I've ever seen."

He cupped her breasts in the palms of his warm hands and gently hefted their weight, before stroking his thumbs across the tips. Her nipples immediately contracted. When he bent his head to kiss her breasts, Jessie pushed her fingers through his short hair, the thick, damp layers cool in comparison to the heat of his scalp. When he raised his head, she pressed a soft, lingering kiss against his mouth.

"Come with me," she urged, and took his hands, before walking backward in the direction of the bed and tugging him with her.

Holt didn't resist.

There was a telltale rise at the front of his boxers, proof of his arousal. The knowledge that she could excite him so gave Jessie added confidence, especially when she recalled how he had rebuffed her efforts to touch him in the barn. When the backs of her thighs bumped against the bed, she drew Holt closer and kissed him again, fusing her mouth with his. His hands came back to her breasts, gently squeezing and fondling them as he kissed her. Desire jackknifed through her and she didn't protest when his hands moved to her waistband and unfastened the snap of her jeans.

"If you're staying, you won't need these," he said. "Take

them off."

His soft order caused shivers of anticipation to course through Jessie. She complied, unzipping her pants and pushing them down over her hips and then toeing her canvas shoes off before she stepped completely out of the jeans. She was trembling inside, half-afraid Holt would change his mind. But instead, he gave a soft laugh and muttered something that sounded suspiciously like *I am so fucked*.

Not yet, Jessie thought with feminine satisfaction, *but soon*.

"Take me to bed, Holt," she commanded, and moved into his arms.

He hauled her against his body until her breasts flattened against his chest, and kissed her until she was breathless. When he eased her back onto the bed, she pulled him with her, loving the heavy weight of him on top of her.

"You're sure about this?" Holt pressed his mouth against the sensitive skin beneath her ear, causing delicious shivers.

"Yes. A thousand times, yes."

As if he only needed that assurance, he kissed her again, before he worked his way down her body, lingering over her breasts and drawing each nipple into his mouth, in turn. Jessie gasped and arched upward, her hands in his hair as he moved lower still and teased the whorl of her navel with his tongue. When he reached the edge of her panties, he glanced up at her, his blue eyes gleaming in the indistinct light.

"I've been wanting to do this since our night in the barn." He slowly drew the scrap of fabric down, until he could pull it completely free of her body.

Our night in the barn.

His words warmed Jessie, doing more to make her feel connected to him than any physical contact could. She had never been so acutely aware of her own vulnerability. She'd wanted Holt for as long as she could remember and now, she was laying herself bare to him, in every way possible. He could break her heart, but it was a risk she was willing to take.

"Holt," she said, reaching for him, "come up here with me."

"In a moment," he murmured, and skated his palms over her thighs before lowering his head and following the path of his hands with his lips. He kissed the inside of her knee and then moved upward, until he was at the apex of her thighs.

"Open up for me, darlin'."

His breath huffed warmly against her sensitive flesh and then his hands were there, gently parting her as he stroked a finger through her feminine folds. Jessie gasped, but any thought of stopping him was obliterated beneath the hot, slick wash of his tongue against her. A small exclamation escaped her and then she stopped thinking completely as he proceeded to make her lose her mind. He licked at her, using his mouth and tongue to drive her need higher. The sight of his broad shoulders and dark head between her thighs was the most erotic thing Jessie had ever seen and her hands clenched convulsively in the bedding as tight coils of tension gathered and built inside her. Reaching up, Holt covered one hand with his own, lacing his fingers with hers.

"Let it go, darlin'," he said.

The sensation of his mouth, combined with his husky command, was more than Jessie could take, and the building pressure shattered and broke over her in powerful waves. Holt didn't stop until the last quiver had subsided from her body and Jessie lay boneless beneath him. Easing himself over her, he kissed her deeply. Jessie reached down and cupped him through the soft fabric of his boxers.

"I want you so much," she murmured against his mouth. "Take these off and come inside me."

Holt dropped his head to her shoulder, his breathing uneven. "I'm sorry, sweetheart. I want to more than I want my next breath. But I can't. I don't have any protection and I won't put you at risk."

It took a moment for Jessie to understand what he was saying. He had invited her to stay, knowing he couldn't finish what he'd started? It was so unlike Holt that she actually found it endearing. "But I thought all guys carried protection."

"I haven't had a reason to," he said, lifting his head and letting her see the regret in his eyes.

"What if I'm safe?" She wound her arms around his neck.

"We can't," he said. "Trust me when I say this is harder for me than it is for you."

Jessie gave a small gurgle of laughter. "Holt Claiborne, did you just make a joke?"

"I'd laugh myself, if I thought it was funny," he groaned.

"Here, roll over." Jessie pushed at his broad shoulders and he complied, rolling onto his back beside her. Hooking

149

her fingers into the waistband of the briefs, she pulled them down. Holt lifted his hips to help her. The light slanting in from the bathroom washed over him, revealing the most perfect physique Jessie had ever seen. Even his thighs were strongly muscled and his other assets—Jessie had known he was large, but seeing his erection made her want to weep with disappointment that they wouldn't be having sex. She trailed her fingers over his stomach, and stroked his shaft. He watched her with molten eyes and bent his arms behind his head, displaying his impressive triceps. He lay quietly, but Jessie wasn't fooled. Even if his body hadn't given him away, the ruddy color on his cheekbones and his agitated breathing would have. It was taking all his restraint to remain pliant and unmoving beneath her roaming hands.

"What did you have in mind?" His eyes glittered as he watched her.

"Just this," she said, and leaned over to kiss him. She used her lips and tongue, making the kiss as lush as she knew how while she continued to stroke and squeeze him, until Holt buried his hands in her hair and sank his tongue deep into her mouth.

Breaking the kiss, she released him, and worked her way down his body, lingering over the flat discs of his nipples and smoothing her palms over his pecs. His stomach muscles contracted as she kissed her way downward, gently biting his hip bone and then curling her hand around his hardness. His breath hissed in as she began to stroke him, but when she touched him with her tongue, he made a deep groaning sound of pleasure. Knowing he watched her, Jessie drew him into her mouth and began to lave him with her tongue, hoping her enthusiasm made up for her limited experience. Holt's body tightened and his breathing grew ragged as she stroked him with her hands and mouth. He caressed her ears, her neck, her shoulders, keeping his touch light and gentle, but Jessie knew the precise moment that he no longer had control over his own reaction.

"Jessica." His voice sounded ragged, urgent. "Are you sure you're safe?"

Jessie raised her head. Holt's blue eyes were unfocused, his color high.

"I've been on the pill since I was seventeen to regulate my periods. I promise you I'm safe."

"Jessie, if we do this—"

She leveraged herself up until she was beside him. "Holt, I've wanted this forever. Please don't make me wait any longer."

In a heartbeat, Jessie found herself on her back beneath him. He hooked his arms beneath her knees and opened her wide. He was looking at her as if he wanted to eat her alive.

"Jess . . ." His voice sounded low and anguished.

"Please, *yes.*"

Almost before the word was uttered, he slid into her in one deep, glorious thrust. Jessie cried out with the sheer intensity of it and her body clenched hard around the wet silken hardness of him. She pulled him down on top of her and kissed him, her arms and legs locked around his taut body as he moved. He slanted his mouth hard across hers, using his teeth and lips and tongue to coax a greedy response from her. Jessie lifted her hips to meet his powerful thrusts, the voluptuous slide of his flesh pulling her into another orgasm. She came in hard shudders and, through a haze of blinding pleasure, watched Holt's legendary control crumble as he came apart in her arms.

He lay still for several long moments with his face against her neck, dragging in deep lungfuls of air. Then he rolled onto his back and tucked her snugly against his side. Jessie curled against him, listening to the strong thud of his heart. His breathing still came in ragged gusts, and she slid an arm and leg across his body, as if she could protect him from himself.

"Good?" she asked softly.

"Honey," he said thickly, "it was good the second you walked into the room. But that—" He gave a soft huff of laughter. "That was worth the wait."

Jessie almost stopped breathing. Carefully, she raised herself on one elbow and studied his face in the dim light. "You've been waiting for me?"

He looked disconcerted for a moment and then seemed to collect himself. "I only meant that I've, uh, gone *without* for a while now." He pulled her onto his chest and bracketed her face in his hands as he kissed her. "But I've only gotten started with you."

Jessie felt her heart hitch. "What did you have in mind?"

"Everything, darlin'," he said in a rough whisper, and kissed her again. "Let me show you."

Chapter Twelve

JESSICA RETURNED TO her own rooms just after dawn. Holt had tried to persuade her to spend the morning in bed with him, but she reminded him that his father and Evan could be home in time for breakfast. He'd reluctantly let her go, knowing his own chores wouldn't wait. Now he lay on his bed, conflicted and filled with doubts. Had the sex been amazing?

Yes.

He told himself sex wasn't enough to sustain a relationship.

But it was a good start, a small voice whispered.

Her fragrance lingered on his skin and his bedding and he had to resist the urge to bury his face in the pillows and inhale. When he closed his eyes, he saw her sprawled across his bed, her face a study in erotic pleasure. With a groan, he sat up on the edge of the mattress and buried his face in his hands.

He was in serious trouble.

He'd completely lost control. No woman had ever driven him to the edge the way Jessica had. He still couldn't wrap his head around the fact that he'd been so absorbed in his own skyrocketing lust for her that he'd been ready to throw all caution aside. He wasn't sure he could have stopped had his life depended on it. He'd gotten lucky when she'd said she was protected, because he wasn't certain it would have mattered to him if she hadn't been. He was thirty-five years old, way past the age where his libido should override his common sense.

He was supposed to be the responsible one, the Claiborne who followed the rules and put the welfare of others first. And yet, he'd put his own urgent need for release ahead of her. There'd been no finesse or tenderness to his lovemaking. In fact, he'd behaved only a little better than one of his bulls. If Jessica had managed to enjoy herself, it wasn't because of anything he had done. He only hoped he'd made up for it afterward, when he'd loved her as gently and tenderly as he could.

He loved her.

Being with Jessica had exceeded every fantasy he'd ever had of her, and he'd had plenty.

A soft noise by the bedroom door alerted Holt and he looked up, hoping it might be Jessie. Instead, Sam nudged his way into the bedroom and padded across the floor to push his wet nose beneath Holt's hand.

"Hey, old boy," he murmured, rubbing the dog's head. "I'm in trouble, aren't I?"

Sam's tail wagged in agreement.

"Okay, first things first. The sooner we get the chores done, the sooner we can be back here. Agreed?"

Sam lay down with a soft grunt and dropped his muzzle

onto his paws. Holt fished a pair of jeans out of his dresser and pulled them on, getting dressed in the predawn darkness. The house was quiet as he made his way downstairs and grabbed a mug of coffee before he headed out to the barns. He went through his morning routine on autopilot, his thoughts consumed with Jessie and how their relationship had taken an unexpected turn.

He'd become so accustomed to keeping people—keeping *her*—at arm's length, that he suddenly found himself floundering, out of his depth. Because despite his intent to keep Jessica Montero at an emotional distance, she had found her way under his skin and into his carefully fortressed heart. Far from being able to push her to the back of his thoughts, she'd grabbed a seat front and center, and he'd be dead before he forgot any part of what they'd shared. Every scorching second was imprinted on his brain and his body.

Worse, he wanted a repeat performance.

"WHERE'S JESSICA?"

Holt finished the morning chores and walked back to the house for breakfast to find Gus and Evan had returned from Fort Worth. Accustomed to seeing Jessie in the kitchen during breakfast, her absence was both disappointing and disquieting.

"She said she had to leave," Evan said, helping himself to a serving of breakfast casserole while Gus buttered a thick, sugar-topped muffin. "But she left this for us."

"Did she say why?"

Gus finished preparing his muffin and carefully poured himself a cup of coffee. When he finally looked at Holt, his expression was a mixture of regret and sympathy. "She gave me her notice, effective immediately."

Holt stared at his father, not sure he understood correctly. "She what?"

"She quit, bro," Evan offered. "She was already packed and waiting to go when we got here. Shit, we leave for one day and you manage to scare her off. What the hell did you do to her?"

Evan's words were like a physical blow. There was no doubt in Holt's mind that she'd left because of him. Because of what had happened. But he didn't understand why, since she'd seemed okay when she'd left him. She'd seemed happy. What had gone wrong?

"Did she leave a message for me?"

"Yes." Gus paused. "She asked for your cell phone number and said she would call you."

"When?"

"I don't know."

For just an instant, Holt felt as bereft as he had on the day his second stepmother, whom he'd affectionately dubbed "Nan," had left them, taking Emmaline with her. He'd adored Nan, but that hadn't mattered. His love hadn't been enough to make her stay at Riverrun Ranch. Aware that his father and brother were watching him, he schooled his features and nodded.

"Okay, thanks. For what it's worth, I'm sorry she's gone.

I was against her coming to the ranch, but I was wrong. She was—" He broke off, unsure how to continue.

"She was pretty damned perfect," Evan grumbled.

"I'm sorry, too, son," Gus said. "I guess it wasn't working out for her. Although I admit, I'm surprised. She seemed happy enough."

"Apparently not."

"If you're really sorry, you'll go over and persuade her to come back," Evan said.

Holt looked at his brother. "What makes you think I'll be able to persuade her?"

Evan shrugged, but his eyes glinted with warm mockery. "Don't tell me you had nothing to do with her leaving, because I'm not buying it."

Had his feelings been that obvious?

"She's a grown woman," he muttered. "She can make her own decisions."

Evan made a snorting sound but didn't reply.

"Are you going to eat?" Gus asked.

"Thanks, but I'm not hungry."

Holt made his way upstairs to shower and change. He'd lost his appetite. He felt the weight of dread like a rock in his stomach. Jessica had tidied his room before she'd left, putting fresh sheets on the bed and clean towels in his bathroom. She'd never done that before and he took it as a good sign that she'd been in his room. He found himself looking for something, anything that might hint as to why she'd left. A note, maybe.

But there was nothing.

WHEN THE DAY wore on and Jessie still hadn't called him, Holt drove over to her house, determined to see her. If she didn't want to be with him, fine, but he needed to hear it from her own lips. He felt anxious and out of sorts in a way that was unfamiliar to him. Despite telling himself there must be a good reason for why she'd left, why she hadn't yet contacted him, anxiety gnawed at him. What if she really didn't want him in her life? The thought was too dismal to even consider.

As if in sympathy with his mood, storm clouds began to gather overhead. The sky turned the color of cigarette smoke and the air grew heavy with heat and moisture. Holt turned down the gravel road that led to Jessie's cabin and parked a little away from the small house. As he climbed the stairs to her door, he heard her voice and realized she was on the outside deck, speaking to someone. He could hear her, but he couldn't see her. Not wanting to intrude, Holt paused for a moment on the stairs, but couldn't help overhearing part of her conversation.

" . . . won't go back to Riverrun unless it's as *Mrs. Claiborne.* That would never have crossed my mind before yesterday, but the more I think about it, the more it makes perfect sense."

Holt froze. Was Jessie talking about herself and *him*?

"You're right," Jessie continued, and Holt realized she was speaking on her phone. "I need the money and if Holt is the key to getting it, then a girl's gotta do what a girl's gotta do, right? Wish me luck."

Holt felt his chest constrict. Did she mean what he thought she meant? He had a difficult time believing Jessica was mercenary, but he'd heard the words straight from her mouth. Not wanting to hear any more, Holt backed quietly down the stairs and returned to his truck, his mind reeling. He had no idea who Jessie was talking to on the phone, but there was no mistaking her meaning.

All this time, she'd been using him.

He felt sick to his stomach.

He sat for a moment, reeling, before he turned the ignition on and thrust the truck into gear, accelerating out of her driveway faster than he should have. At the end of the drive, he didn't slow down and was nearly broadsided by another pickup truck traveling on the main road. The driver laid on his horn and Holt stomped down hard on the brakes and came to a lurching stop. His heart pounded hard in his chest and it had nothing to do with the near collision. Jessica's words continued to echo in his head.

I need money and if Holt is the key to getting it, then a girl's gotta do what a girl's gotta do.

She thought by duping him into marrying her, she could also have access to his bank account. How was she planning to persuade him? By pretending to love him? Was that why she had left without a word? To make him miss her so much that he'd do anything to have her back?

Even marry her?

Checking the traffic, Holt pulled onto the main road and drove toward town. He couldn't return to Riverrun Ranch, at least not until he'd had time to process what he'd overheard. He still couldn't quite believe it. Jessica had never struck him as a material girl, obsessed with things or money. In fact, her down-to-earth simplicity was one of the things he loved best about her. There was never any pretense with her—at least, that's what he had believed.

There had to be some misunderstanding, but the more Holt replayed the scene in his mind, the more he became convinced he was the one who had misunderstood who Jessie really was. All this time, he'd thought she was different when, in fact, she was exactly like his ex-wife. The worst part was that he *had* been thinking about marrying her. He loved her. He didn't want to spend his life without her. He should feel grateful that he'd learned the truth now, instead of later, but his heart felt broken. His chest actually ached in the center, like he'd been back-kicked by one of his bulls.

He gripped the steering wheel so tightly, his knuckles turned white. He couldn't remember the last time he'd been this upset. When he reached the downtown area, he pulled into an empty parking spot in front of Kolaches. He had some idea of going in for coffee and a bite to eat but remembering the last time he had been here—with Jessie—made him hesitate. In all likelihood, he wouldn't be able to eat a bite. A light knock on the window startled him and he looked around to see his brother Luke standing beside the truck, grinning at him.

Holt put his window down. "Hey, what's up?"

Luke nodded toward the bakery. "Jorie's inside getting us a table. Why don't you join us?"

Holt hadn't seen Luke in several days, but he wasn't sure he'd be good company. "I don't know. I don't want to be a third wheel."

Luke's eyebrows shot up. "Seriously, bro? Don't be a douche. Come have breakfast with us or I'll think you don't like my girlfriend."

Holt did like Jorie. She was sweet and unpretentious and had overcome the many obstacles in her life with a cheerful determination. More importantly, she made his brother happy and together they'd made a nice life for themselves, running the wildlife rehab center and a canine training school. Holt wouldn't want either of them to think he had any issues with their relationship.

"Okay," he relented. "But fair warning—I'm not in a great mood today."

Luke laughed. "How would anyone know?"

Holt frowned, but followed his brother into the restaurant, removing his hat and smoothing his hair before threading his way through the tables to a corner booth where Jorie waited for them. She stood up and he gave her a brief hug before sliding into the booth across from her and Luke.

"This is a nice surprise," Jorie said, smiling.

Holt forced himself to be sociable. "Yeah, it's good to see you, Jorie. How's everything over at the rehab center?"

"We had an injured fox brought in last night. She'd been caught in a trap, but I think she'll make a full recovery." She frowned. "When are people going to stop setting foothold traps out of season? They're dangerous and illegal. I've already notified Chief Highwater, so hopefully his officers will patrol the back roads more often for poachers."

Holt exchanged an amused look with Luke. Jorie was a force of nature when it came to protecting wildlife. They placed their lunch orders and Holt wrapped his hands around his coffee mug, hoping he sounded casual.

"Have you seen or talked to Jessie recently?" He glanced at Jorie. The two women were best friends. If anyone knew about her plans, she would.

"Not recently. Why?" Jorie's attention sharpened on him. "Is everything okay?"

Holt lifted a shoulder. "Sure. I mean, she's fine, if that's what you're asking."

Luke's eyes narrowed. "Something you're not telling us?"

Holt blew out a hard breath. He needed a sounding board but he'd never been good at opening up and talking about his feelings. The best he could do was give them the bare facts. "She left the ranch this morning without warning."

Luke and Jorie exchanged a meaningful glance. "Why? Is Rosa-Maria okay?"

"Yes, at least, I think so." He risked a glance at Jorie. "I won't go into details, but it's unlikely she'll return to River-run. It's probably for the best."

Jorie dug through her tote bag and pulled out her cell phone. "Let me give her a call and find out what's going on."

Reaching over, Holt covered her hand with his own. "Not now, Jorie. Later, okay?"

Jorie's expression reflected her confusion and her concern. "What is it, Holt? Did something happen between the two of you? I probably shouldn't say this, but that girl has been crazy about you for years. She was so excited about coming to the ranch because she was finally going to have the chance to get to know you better."

Holt's mouth flattened. "Mission accomplished. Let's just say she had me fooled about the kind of person she really is."

An astonished laugh escaped Jorie. "I know Jessie better than anyone. We've been friends since we were about ten years old and I'm telling you she is the sweetest, most loyal friend I've ever had. Do you think Emmaline would be friends with her if she were a deceitful person?" She gave him a disapproving frown. "Shame on you, Holt Claiborne."

Her censure made Holt feel about six inches tall. "I hope like hell I'm wrong about this. I want to be wrong, but I just came from her house, and it sure seems like I was right." As both Luke and Jorie continued to stare at him in disbelief, he pulled his wallet out and tossed several bills onto the table. "I warned you I wouldn't be good company, so I think it's better if I just leave. I wasn't that hungry to begin with."

"You don't need to leave," Luke protested.

Holt got up and stood there for a moment with his hat in his hands. "If you do see Jessica, tell her I'm sorry things didn't work out."

He turned and made his way blindly out of the restaurant. Luke caught up with him beside his truck.

"Hey, are you okay?" His dark eyes mirrored his concern.

Holt paused with his hand on the door handle. "I took her to bed last night."

Luke gave him a baffled look and shrugged. "Okay, anyone could see that one coming, no pun intended. So why all the drama today?"

Holt shook his head. "It was bad."

Luke gave him an astonished look. "What do you mean *bad*? As in the worst sex you've ever had? Maybe she's just inexperienced. You can always work on that."

"I wish." Holt groaned and pinched the bridge of his nose. "No, the sex was unbelievable, but I, ah, wasn't in control, at least initially. I didn't have any protection and I didn't even care. She said she's on the pill, but I have no idea if that's true. I just trusted her."

Luke's expression cleared and he grinned. "Ah . . . the mighty Holt discovers he is human, after all."

"Okay, you know what? Forget it. I shouldn't have said anything."

Luke laughed, but stepped between Holt and the truck, preventing him from opening the driver's-side door. "Sorry, bro, but you have to see how amusing this is."

"Not seeing it."

"C'mon, you've been so determined to remain single, when everyone in town could see how you feel about Jessie."

"I barely talked to her before she came to work at the ranch!"

"But you've been going to the cantina every Thursday night for years. People notice."

Holt muttered a curse under his breath. "This is not helpful."

"So why won't you let Jessie come back to the ranch?" Luke's tone was gentle. "If last night was so great, why don't you want to see her again?"

Holt blew out a hard breath. "I went over to her place this morning to talk to her and inadvertently overheard a conversation she was having with someone on the phone. She said—*clearly*—that she wouldn't return to the ranch unless it was as *my wife*. She went on to say that she needs money and I'm the key to her getting it." Seeing Luke's disbelief, he shrugged. "I heard her say it, Luke."

"Are you in love with her?" The question was direct and blunt.

He was in love with her but a relationship based on lies and greed could only end badly. He'd done that once. No way would he do it again. He needed to protect what was left of his heart.

"What does it matter?" He avoided the question. "I was wrong about her."

"You just told me you trusted her last night. Why can't you trust her now?"

"You didn't hear her. How can I be with a woman who's only after my money?"

Luke narrowed his eyes. "I seem to recall another occasion when you misjudged someone. Before you do anything you'll regret, talk to Jessie. I feel pretty sure there's a good explanation for whatever you think you heard."

Luke was referring to Cort, and Holt's early condemnation of him when he'd believed the younger man was trying to swindle Emmaline out of her inheritance. He'd been wrong about that, much to everyone's relief.

"I'll talk to her, but I don't think it's going to make a difference."

Chapter Thirteen

HOLT WAS IN deep shit, literally.

He was in the breeding barn, checking the progress of each pregnant cow. Beside him, Cort held a cow's tail aside while Holt stood behind the animal, wearing an arm-length glove as he carefully palpated the cow's uterus, feeling for the unborn calf. After a moment, he grinned at Cort.

"Twins."

"Nice."

Holt withdrew his arm and was stripping the glove off when a shadow fell across his feet.

"Here you are. I've been looking for you."

Holt turned. Jessie stood several feet away, and he didn't need to be a genius to tell she was angry. She wore a pair of shorts with Western boots and a loose, flowery top, and her hair hung in a single, dark braid over her shoulder. He wished to hell she didn't look so good. Less than a day had passed since he'd overheard the conversation on her deck. He'd planned to return to her house that afternoon to talk with her. But he hadn't.

"I'll, uh, just put momma cow back with the others,"

Cort said, glancing uneasily between the two of them. Without waiting for a response, he led the cow to the back of the enormous barn where the pens were located.

"Bring me out another one," Holt called after him. He discarded the soiled glove and angled his head to look at Jessie as he walked over to the indoor sink to wash his hands. "I was going to stop by your place later."

"Why? To accuse me of wanting your money?" Her expressive eyes flashed fire at him and her entire body was rigid with suppressed emotion. He guessed that Luke had talked to Jorie, who had, in turn, talked to Jessie. So now she knew that he was onto her plan to marry him for his money. Even after finding out she wasn't what he'd thought her to be, he had to admit her outrage seemed genuine. He just wished his heart didn't react so strongly to the sight of her. There was a part of him that longed to tell her he didn't care why she wanted him, as long as she wanted him. She could have anything—a ring, his money, the whole enchilada, if she would just look at him the way she had that night.

Drying his hands, he picked up the clipboard he'd been using to annotate the results of the examinations and made his own pretense of being absorbed in writing. "Do you deny it?"

"You're damned right I deny it! Do you really believe I'm after your money? That I have some"—she gestured with her hands—"some devious plan to trick you into marrying me so that I can get my hands on your money?"

Holt lowered the clipboard and looked at her. "Don't you?"

"No! Honestly, Holt, it isn't like you to jump to conclusions. Whatever you believe, you're wrong."

"I know what I overheard, Jessica."

"Oh, really? Tell me," she demanded. "Tell me what you think you heard."

Holt blew out a hard breath. "You said you wouldn't return to the ranch unless it was as *Mrs. Claiborne*."

Jessie recoiled and her expression turned to one of disbelief. "That conversation was private and—by the way—had absolutely nothing to do with you! Are you really so arrogant as to believe every woman who shows an interest in you wants to marry you?"

Holt stiffened. "I also heard you say that you needed money and I was the key to getting it."

Jessie crossed her arms and stared him down. "Yes, I did say that."

"So I was right."

To his astonishment, her expression softened. The anger seemed to slip away, replaced with something like exasperation and affection.

"No, Holt, you couldn't be more wrong." She stepped toward him, lowering her voice. "I was talking about my *grandmother*. She loves your father, but they've had some kind of falling out. When I asked if she might be interested in moving back to the ranch, she said she would only return to Riverrun as your *father's* wife!" She paused. "If you're still not sure, ask my mother, she was there. Ask Rosa-Maria. I'm sure she'd tell you the truth. Better yet, ask Gus. I think that's what they argued about and why he won't see her. He refuses to get married again because he's too afraid of getting hurt." A faint smile crossed her face. "Like father, like son, apparently."

Holt frowned, feeling more and more foolish in the face of her reasonable explanation. "What about the money? I didn't mistake that."

"Actually, you did. My grandmother told me how you've invested her money for her all these years and that she's accumulated a nice nest egg. She wants me to use part of it to purchase my food truck."

Holt shook his head. "No, that's not what I heard."

"She also told me that if I want the money, I'd need to speak to you about it because you manage the account. That's what you heard, Holt. You're the key to releasing my grandmother's funds. But if you still don't believe me, talk to Emmaline. She was the one on the phone with me that morning."

Holt swore beneath his breath. "Jessica, I don't know what to say. I've been an ass."

"Yes, you have."

Holt spread his hands out. "I'm sorry."

"Oh, no." Jessie put her hands up and took a step backward. "You do not get to apologize and all is forgiven. I mean, I'll probably forgive you eventually, because I actually understand how you might have misread the situation, but right now I am still furious that you would think that about me. That you could actually believe me capable of something so cold. Especially after—"

She broke off.

"Jessica—"

"You believed the worst of me, Holt, but you know what hurts the most?" She didn't give him a chance to reply as she plunged on. "I've been crazy about you for a long time and the other night was like a dream come true. It was beyond amazing. I gave you a part of myself that I've never shared with anyone: my heart. I love you, Holt Blaisdell Claiborne, but I'm not like my grandmother. I'm not going to hang around for another twenty years, waiting for you to decide whether or not you want me in your life."

Holt felt gutted by her words, his mind reeling. A hard ache formed in the center of his chest and he had to resist the urge to rub the area. "Jessica, tell me what I need to do to make this right. Please." He wanted to tell her he loved her, too, but found he couldn't form the words. "I do want you in my life," he said, instead.

She considered him for a moment. "Woo me, Holt. If that's true, then show me. Make it public and take me on a date. I want an old-fashioned courtship, and you don't even need to spend a penny."

"Woo you?" Holt stared at her. "I'm not even sure I know what that means."

"You'll figure it out." She gave him a small smile. "See you later."

He watched as she turned and left the barn, and then followed her to the open doors. Jessie walked toward the house, her head high. She didn't look back once.

"You okay?"

Holt turned to see Cort standing several feet away,

watching him. His face was carefully impassive, but there was no mistaking the humor and empathy in his eyes.

Holt dragged in a deep breath and blew it out hard. "I have no fucking clue what to do."

Cort rubbed a hand across the back of his neck. "I once rode a bull named Nitroglycerin. That son of a bitch had a reputation as a rank, unrideable monster. I very nearly quit bull riding that day, that's how scared I was. But I'd drawn his name, and if I wanted to realize my dream, I had no choice but to climb on and hope for the best. I was just twenty-one and I didn't really care if I couldn't stick for eight seconds—I knew I wouldn't. I just needed to survive the ride, however short it might be."

"Is there a point to this story?"

Cort seemed unfazed by Holt's impatience. "That bull exploded out of the chute with me on his back and then proceeded to run around the arena, but he never got his ass into the air." He paused. "It was the best and worst ride of my career. The best, because I stayed on past the eight-second buzzer and the worst because, for the next month, I felt like the laughingstock of the circuit. They retired Nitro-glycerin shortly after that. He never bucked again."

Holt regarded the other man with a steady look, wondering how the story was relevant. "That's, uh, very interesting."

Cort grinned. "I learned a lot from that ride. Expect the unexpected. Whatever you think will happen, be prepared for the opposite." He tipped his hat back on his head. "You're expecting to get bucked off and busted up, but instead you find yourself on the softest, sweetest ride of your life. Theoretically speaking, of course. But you'll never know which way it's going to go until you climb on." He skewered Holt with a direct look. "I wasted unnecessary time worrying about that damned ride. Don't let fear hold you back, Holt. Don't quit just because you're afraid the ride will be rough. Maybe you'll be surprised."

"Or maybe I'll be a laughingstock."

"I got over it," Cort said drily. "So will you."

Holt hesitated. "She wants me to *woo* her."

Cort laughed. "You'll do great."

"I've never courted a woman."

"Use your imagination. What do women like?" Cort began to check off on his fingers. "Flowers. Picnics. Surprise drives through the country. Lemonade and porch swings. Impulsive gestures. Lots of kissing."

"I've never been the impulsive kind," Holt complained.

"Maybe you should try it."

"Bring me another cow," he told Cort. "Let's get this finished."

Cort looked at him with something like disappointment in his eyes. "Sure," he said, but as he turned away, he said something under his breath that sounded suspiciously like *Coward.*

⚸

HAD SHE OVERREACTED?

Driving back to her own house, Jessie's thoughts replayed the scene in the barn again and again. In all fairness, she understood how Holt might have misunderstood what he'd overheard. Considering his first wife had put him through hell, his suspicion was understandable. But Jessie couldn't get past the hurt of knowing he'd thought the worst about her. At the very least, he could have confronted her and given her the chance to explain herself instead of leaping to conclusions. That's what stung the most—that she'd opened herself to him body and heart, yet he didn't trust her.

But he had apologized, she reminded herself. And his distress had seemed sincere. She recalled again the look in his eyes when she'd told him she wouldn't wait around for him to make up his mind about her. For just an instant, he'd looked completely devastated. It had taken everything Jessie had not to run into his arms and tell him she would never, ever leave him.

She groaned, remembering what she had said to him. She'd told him *she loved him.* She'd put her feelings out there and the best he could do was to say he wanted her in his life. She'd left, half hoping he would chase after her, but he hadn't. Would he accept her challenge to woo her? She liked the idea of Holt showing up in his truck with a handful of wildflowers. If he really cared enough about her, he needed to show it. She was done pursuing him.

As she drove through town, she made a spur-of-the-moment decision and pulled into the bank parking lot. She would request a loan for the food truck and finally move forward with that dream. She didn't want to wait another year to save the money and she didn't want to take any of her grandmother's precious savings. She preferred to be master of her own destiny and this would ensure she wouldn't have to ask Holt for anything.

Thirty minutes later, having secured a preapproval for the loan, Jessie returned to her vehicle. All that was required was for her to drive over to the dealership and sign the paperwork. The food truck could be hers before the end of the day. She'd need to make some sacrifices in order to afford the payment, but she hoped those would only be temporary and that her business would soon pay for itself. She sat for a moment in her Jeep and let the enormity of what she'd done sink in. Her dream of becoming an entrepreneur was within her grasp. Everything was falling into place. Well, everything except for what she'd wanted for the longest time—Holt Claiborne. She should be happy, but instead she wanted to cry.

As if in sympathy with her dismal mood, fat raindrops began to plop onto her windshield. Glancing upward, she saw the skies were dark with storm clouds. Maybe she would wait until the next day to visit the dealership. The truck would still be there tomorrow, and she could spend today finalizing the many other things that needed to be done before she could actually get her business on the road.

By the time she arrived at her house, the rain had intensified and thunder rumbled ominously overhead. Jessie made a dash for the cottage, sprinting up the stairs to the deck and wasting precious seconds unlocking the door. By the time she was finally inside, she was soaked through. She changed into dry clothes and stood by the French doors that led to her deck, watching the rain pelt the glass. Beyond the deck, the waters of the Pedernales River churned past, stirred to a muddy brown by the deluge. Jessie had placed four lawn chairs and a low table on the grass near the riverbank and she considered dragging them to higher ground in case the water rose. Even as she walked toward the closet for her rain jacket, her phone began to ring. Her heart skipped a beat and she couldn't suppress the hope that it might be Holt.

"Hey, Jessie, it's me."

"Emmaline, hi." She paused, guessing the reason for her friend's phone call. "Cort told you what happened."

"Are you okay?"

"As well as can be expected, considering I pretty much gave Holt an ultimatum with no guarantee he'll do what I want." Jessie sighed deeply before walking into her living room and making herself comfortable on the couch. "I still can't believe he thought I wanted to marry him for his money. Was I wrong to confront him?"

"*No.* He needs to know he's not always right and that he makes mistakes just like the rest of us mortals."

Jessie smiled reluctantly. "I'm sure he hates that."

"Well, it wouldn't be the first time Holt has misread a situation. He all but threw Cort out of the house last year because he thought he was after my money. See a theme here?"

"Well, he admitted he was mistaken about Cort, and he apologized for jumping to conclusions about me," Jessie said.

"I'm sure he feels terrible about what happened. I have a feeling you'll be seeing him sooner than later. Holt's a smart guy and he's not going to let you get away."

Jessie wished she could be so sure, but she didn't say so to Emmaline.

"Thanks, I appreciate the call."

"You sound a little down. I can come over if you'd like."

"I'm okay," Jessie fibbed. "I actually stopped by the bank on my way home and got approved for a loan."

"Finally! Jessie, that's wonderful."

They talked for a few minutes longer until Jessie had convinced Emmaline that she was doing just fine.

Even if it wasn't the truth.

Outside, the rain continued to beat at the windows.

Chapter Fourteen

FOUR HOURS AFTER Jessie left Riverrun Ranch, the rain still cascaded down. Holt and Cort stood inside the barn and watched the deluge. Lightning flashed overhead, followed by yet another crack of thunder. They had finished examining each of the pregnant cows and were now debating whether or not to make a run for the house.

"This isn't clearing up anytime soon," observed Holt. "I have some paperwork I can finish up here."

"Glad we moved the cattle to high ground yesterday," Cort commented. "You were right about the storm."

"Yeah, well, that's the only thing I've been right about lately." His voice was terse.

The sound of a phone ringing distracted them. Holt pulled his mobile phone out of a pocket and glanced at it before answering, trying not to let his disappointment show. It wasn't Jessie, although he hadn't really expected her to call him. The next move was on him if he wanted to make things right with her.

"Hey, Evan, you okay? I thought you'd be back by now." He could barely hear his brother on the other end of the connection but what he did hear galvanized him into action.

"Hang on. We'll be there as soon as we can!"

"What's going on?" Cort's attention was riveted on him.

"Evan found a cluster of cattle in the low pasture, near the river. They're on the wrong side of the fence and the water is rising. They knocked down the fence trying to escape and now they're tangled in wire. Evan needs help cutting them free."

"Let's go," Cort said.

He and Cort threw on their rain gear, saddled their horses, and loaded wire cutters and extra gloves into the saddlebags. They rode through the torrential downpour toward the low pasture. The weather forced them to go slowly, picking their way through the gullies of water and eddies of mud toward the spot where Evan said he had found the cattle. At one point, the trail had been washed out, forcing them to seek an alternate route. They rode instead along a ridge that paralleled the river and, even through the driving rain, Holt could see the current was swift.

"There he is!" Cort shouted and pointed toward a copse of trees near a bend in the river.

They picked their way down the ridge, the horses sliding on the slick ground. When they reached the bottom, Holt assessed the situation. Evan's horse stood about fifty yards away, loosely tethered to a shrub. Nearby, a dozen cattle had found their way onto the wrong side of the wire fencing and had become trapped between the rising water and the barbed-wire barrier. In their panic, they had dragged the wire down and four cows were caught in the tangle of metal and wood. Holt could just see Evan in the middle of the mess, cutting wire as rain sheeted down.

An uprooted tree lay beside him and the thick foliage made access to the small herd all but impossible. They would need to cut the fencing away to free the trapped animals, as well as provide them with an escape route.

Dismounting, Holt and Cort secured their horses alongside Evan's and retrieved their wire cutters. One cow was on her side on the ground with barbed wire encircling her feet and hindquarters. Evan had one knee on her neck to prevent her from rising as he worked to cut her loose. Three more cows had the same length of wire coiled around their legs. If they became spooked and tried to bolt, they would not only injure the cow on the ground, but possibly Evan too. All it would take was a sudden crack of thunder or a bolt of lightning to turn the situation deadly.

"Cort, hold this wire for me," Holt directed, and as the other man held the sharp barbs safely aside, Holt climbed through the fencing and knelt on the opposite side of the cow. Water squelched around him and Holt guessed it was about six inches deep and rising fast. The cow's eyes rolled back as he hunkered by her side and her breath came in gusty snorts. She was covered in mud and manure and the wire was so badly snarled around her that Holt knew Evan couldn't have freed her before the water came up and threatened to drown her.

As if reading his thoughts, Evan lifted his head and through the water that gushed off his hat, gave Holt a grateful look. "I sure am glad to see you, brother. Looks like one of the dams let go upriver, or they had to open a sluice gate. We don't have much time."

"We'll get it done," Holt said, but knew Evan was right. He ran his gloved hand over the animal's side, trying to calm her as he gauged where best to cut the wire. "I'm going to release the pressure here. That way if those other cows spook, they won't drag this one—and us—clear across the pasture."

"I'll work on the others," Cort called, and stepped over to where the remaining three cows had been hobbled by the fencing. He moved slowly and spoke in low, soothing tones as he approached them, until finally he could grasp the snarled barbed wire in one hand and begin carefully snipping it away.

While Evan worked to cut the wire away from the cow's front legs, Holt released the fencing from where it twisted around the cow's back legs, carefully pulling it away from the animal until finally, she was free.

"Heads up!" Holt cried as the cow kicked madly, made a deep grunting sound and heaved herself to her feet. Holt pointed to the length of fence that lay on the ground near Evan. "Cut that wire or they're just going to get tangled up again!"

Because of the fallen tree limbs, Evan was the only one who could easily reach the section of fence that had been trampled and broken by the panicked cows. His movements were deft as he snipped back the wire and created an opening through which the cows could escape. Holt moved to help Cort free the other cows and then stepped quickly back as they pulled the wire away and the animals made a break for freedom.

"Okay, boys, let's get them to high ground!" Holt called, gathering the loose wire and wrapping it around one of the fence posts.

Cort and Evan used their hands to wave the cows through the opening and then followed them to ensure they didn't backtrack. Holt bent to retrieve his wire cutters when a movement caught his attention. A calf floundered in the watery muck, her big, dark eyes mirroring her terror. He'd missed seeing her, half-hidden as she was behind a fallen tree limb. Holt slogged his way over to her and, as she struggled to stand, he had to partially dig her back legs out of the quagmire that threatened to keep her trapped and drown her.

"It's okay, darlin'," he said soothingly as he wrestled the baby heifer out of the mud. "I've got you."

Exhausted by the effort to free herself, her legs wobbled and then buckled. Holt lifted her into his arms, holding her securely as he picked his way through the debris and made his way back to his horse. He noted with increasing concern that the water had risen nearly a foot since he and Cort had arrived and there was no sign of the rain letting up.

"I'll bring this one back to the barn," he called to Evan. "You and Cort take the others to high ground."

Evan gave him a thumbs-up and Holt settled the calf across his horse's neck before swinging himself into the saddle and shifting the baby cow to a more secure position across his thighs. He turned back toward the ranch, using one hand to keep the calf in place. The rain hadn't let up in intensity and visibility was poor, making the return trip even slower. He was soaked through to his skin and covered in equal parts mud and manure, but he didn't mind. This was the part of ranching he liked best, when he was in the saddle and making a difference. He didn't even mind that he'd need to go back out and repair the damaged fencing. Since it was already getting dark, he'd wait until morning to take care of that chore, if the water allowed him to get that close.

When the ranch finally came into sight, he turned his horse toward the breeding barn and walked the big chestnut gelding right inside. Sliding from the saddle, he pulled the calf down and carried her over to the pens where he kept the pregnant cows. Setting her inside, he used a towel to rub her down and then prepared a quart of warm milk replacement. She'd need to be bottle-fed until they could reunite her with the momma cow. The calf latched on to the bottle and Holt chuckled as she enthusiastically drained the contents.

"There you go," he said, when the bottle was empty. He gave her an armful of alfalfa and, satisfied that she was warm and comfortable, led Chaos back to the horse barn. He spent another half hour unsaddling his horse and rubbing him down, and then ensuring all the horses had feed and water.

He was preparing to turn out the lights and make a run for the main house when Evan and Cort appeared, leading their horses into the barn.

"It's getting worse out there," Evan said, removing his hat and shaking the excess water from it. "If that river surges, we could see a lot of damage."

"I'm gonna head home," Cort said. "I don't like leaving Emmaline alone during storms like this."

Holt gave the younger man an approving glance. There had been a time when he'd been convinced Cort's intentions toward Emmaline had been less than honorable. The thought made him feel ashamed now, because he'd rarely seen a couple more in love than Cort and Emmaline, unless it was Luke and Jorie. He might have felt jealous if they hadn't been his own family.

"If we lose power, come up to the house," he said. "The generator will be working and we have plenty of room."

"Because Jess is gone and the apartment is empty. You're an idiot, you know that?" Evan yanked the saddle from his horse and hung it over a stand, before hanging the wet pad on a nearby hook. Leading his horse into a stall, he removed the bridle and then came back out to hang it on the wall. "I liked having Jess around and she's a damned good cook. Why'd you have to go and ruin it?"

"She had her reasons for wanting to leave."

"Sure she did." Evan made a scoffing sound, clearly not believing him. "I never took you for a stupid man, so you should probably go after her and make things right."

"I intend to. She said I need to woo her. She wants an old-fashioned courtship."

"Then give that to her." Evan stopped and put his hands on his hips as he stared at Holt. "It's not that hard, bro. Your job is to make her understand what a dumbass you've been and then convince her that you've come to your senses and realize you can't live without her."

"Oh, yeah?" Holt stared at his brother. "If it's so damned easy, why don't you have a girlfriend?"

Evan grinned and began filling a feed bucket with a fragrant mixture of oats and grains. "That's by choice. I have plenty of female companionship, and if I ever wanted to become exclusive, I could do it in a heartbeat."

"Uh-huh, sure. I'd like to see that."

"Well, don't hold your breath. I'm enjoying the bachelor life too much to commit to anyone."

"Someday," said Cort, taking the feed bucket from him and hanging it over his own horse's stall, "some girl is going to walk into your life and *bam*! Your bachelor days are going to be history. You'll never know what hit you."

Evan laughed and began filling a second feed bucket. "That will never happen. If I decide to become exclusive with anyone—and that's a huge if—it will be on my terms. No female is going to control my life, not like you pansies."

This time it was Cort who laughed. He gave Evan a friendly slap on his back. "Sure. You just keep telling yourself that. But I hope to hell I'm around when it happens to you."

Evan scowled and turned away to hang the feed bucket in his horse's stall. He muttered something that sounded suspiciously like *When hell freezes over* and Holt exchanged a grin with Cort.

They left the barn, snapping the lights off and sliding the big door closed. Cort headed toward his truck as Holt and Evan jogged across the soggy grass toward the house. Evan reached out and put a hand on Holt's arm, stopping him.

"Look at that!"

Holt peered through the sheeting rain and saw the river had overflowed its banks. The long expanse of property behind the main house was now completely underwater. The river itself was churning and rushing at a furious rate, more than it had been when they'd rescued the cows. He moved closer and as his eyes adjusted to the dark, he could see the current carried debris with it, fallen trees and logs that the high water had dislodged from the embankments.

Running for the covered porch, he pulled his phone out and called Emmaline. She answered on the first ring.

"Holt? Is everything okay?"

"Yeah, Cort should be home shortly. We found a small herd of cattle stranded by the rising water and had to get them to higher ground, or he'd have already been home."

"Oh, good. I wondered where he was. What's up?"

"Do you have Jessica's phone number?"

"Uh, yes." She gave him the number and Holt committed it to memory. "Can I ask what's going on?"

"I'm worried about her. Do you know if she's at home or with her parents?"

"I talked with her earlier and I think she was at her own place. Why?"

Holt sensed his sister's anxiety. "The river is surging, but I'm hoping she's fine. I'll give her a call to be sure."

"Thank you, Holt. And for what it's worth—" She broke off.

"I'm listening."

"I probably shouldn't say anything, but she's pretty upset."

Holt was silent for a moment. "I know. I'm going to fix it."

"I hope so," Emmaline said.

Holt hung up and immediately dialed Jessica's number, frustrated when it went to voice mail.

"Jessica," he said. "This is Holt. The river is rising and I'm worried about you. Call me to let me know you're okay." He paused. "For what it's worth, the other night was amazing for me too. That's it. . . call me."

He hung up feeling a little foolish, more than a little frustrated, and hopeful that he would hear from her soon. If she didn't return his call, he'd go find her.

Chapter Fifteen

F OR JESSIE, COOKING was both comforting and therapeutic. From the time she'd been old enough to hang out at the cantina with her father, she'd had a fascination with creating food that tasted delicious. But it was her grandmother who had taught her to cook with love and who had shared her recipes with Jessie. As the rain continued to drum down on the roof and pelt against the windows, Jessie prepared her own version of comfort food, *pan de elota*, a sweet corn bread that could pass as a dessert. Those who knew her also knew it was her go-to food whenever she felt stressed or unhappy. Tonight, however, the familiar routine of preparing the favorite dish did nothing to soothe her frayed nerves or her aching heart. Checking that her oven was ready, she scraped the batter into a pan. As she did so, the lights in the kitchen flickered.

"No, no," she said, setting the bowl down. She had just enough time to grab a flashlight from a nearby drawer before the lights went out for good. "Damn."

Switching the flashlight on, she peered out the window, but the darkness was absolute. She couldn't see anything beyond the water that sheeted down the outside of the glass.

Had the entire town lost power, or only her small lane? The other cottages weren't occupied, so there was no one in the vicinity to turn to.

Grabbing her raincoat, she slipped it on and stepped onto the deck that overlooked the river. At first, she couldn't comprehend what she was seeing. The Pedernales River, which was normally twenty feet away from the cottage, was now swirling around and beneath the small structure. The pilings that were meant to keep the house above the flood level had all but disappeared beneath the churning water. In all the years she had lived in Last Stand, the river had never flooded like this.

As she pointed the beam of light into the muddy water, the deck suddenly shifted beneath her feet, causing her to lurch unsteadily and clutch the railing to keep her balance. An enormous log, swept along by the current, had struck one of the support posts beneath the cabin. Jessie couldn't be certain, but she thought the piling had actually snapped beneath the impact.

She needed to leave. *Now.*

Returning to the cottage, she grabbed her car keys and her purse, frantically trying to think of what else she should do. She turned off the oven, just in case the power did return and went back onto the deck. But the stairs that led down to the gravel driveway were submerged and the water was rising fast.

So fast.

Even now, it covered the top step and lapped at the edge of the deck, pushing forward like the incoming tide until the cold water enveloped her feet. Gauging the distance between the house and her Jeep, Jessie briefly considered risking it. She was a strong swimmer, but even the Jeep would soon be underwater. Peering through the deluge, she could see debris in the water. Logs, downed trees and even a piece of lawn furniture swept past the cottage. Trying to swim through that would be foolish, even potentially deadly.

She glanced upward, blinking as the sheeting rain struck her face. How long before the cottage was underwater or, worse, torn free from its support posts and flung into the current? The river would carry it downstream and, even if the little house managed to stay intact, there was a bridge farther down the river that would smash it apart.

Trying not to panic, Jessie retreated into the cottage. She closed the door behind her, but dark water began to seep in over the threshold and spread across the kitchen floor. Pulling out her mobile phone, she dialed 911 with fingers that trembled, grateful when a dispatcher answered on the second ring.

"Last Stand Police Department, please state your emergency."

"Hi, it's Jessie Montero and I'm trapped in my house by the river," she said desperately. "The water is rising fast and I can't get to my car. Please send someone quickly!"

"What's the address, ma'am?"

Jessie gave the woman the street address, adding, "The road is completely underwater. I don't know how you're going to reach me."

"Ma'am, try to stay calm. We'll have someone out to you

as soon as possible. Is there a safe place you can go where the water won't reach you?"

"I don't think so," Jessie said, looking frantically around the small cottage. "Maybe the roof, but I'm terrified the house will be pulled off its support posts. Please hurry!"

"Hold tight, ma'am. Someone will be there soon."

As Jessie ended the call, she saw she had two missed calls from Holt. Worse, the phone was almost out of battery power. Water was now pouring in around the kitchen door and swirling around her ankles. Peering through the window, she could see the water level had reached the bottom of the windows. If she didn't leave the cottage soon, she might not be able to get out at all.

What if the first responders couldn't reach her? What if the cottage was swept away? Would she be safer inside or on the roof? She couldn't think straight. She needed to hear Holt's voice. She needed to make things right with him in case things went very wrong and rescue became impossible. At the very least, she needed to tell Holt how she felt about him. With shaking hands, she pressed his number. The phone rang twice and Jessie sagged with relief when she heard his voice on the other end.

"Jessica! Where are you?"

"I'm at my house and the water is up to the windows! I can't get to my car, Holt. I called 911, but I don't know if they'll be able to reach me. The river is rising fast!"

"Can you get onto the roof?"

"I don't know! I think so, if I climb onto the deck railing."

"Try, sweetheart, but only if you can do it safely. Otherwise, stay inside. I'm on my way."

Her cell phone beeped, signaling the battery was almost drained.

"Holt!"

"I'm here."

"Holt, about what happened—"

"Jessica, sweetheart, tell me when I have you safe in my arms."

Jessie gave a choked laugh that was half sob. "Promise you'll get here soon. I love you—"

With a last warning beep, the phone went dead.

"Holt!" she shouted, but there was only silence and the sound of trickling water as it continued to find its way through the cracks around the door. Overhead, rain drummed on the roof. Just the thought of opening the door and trying to navigate her way through the dark, knee-deep water terrified her. As she peered through the glass, she could see dark objects floating past the deck and the knowledge that the water could soon rise above the windows made her feel panicky. Her opportunity to climb to the roof was quickly disappearing.

At that moment, something big and heavy thudded against the house and made it shake. Jessie grabbed at the counter for balance, terrified the cottage would be ripped from the pilings. She was very close to losing it. People died in floods every year and while she'd heard that death by drowning was a peaceful way to go, the thought of being engulfed in the murky, cold river water terrified her. She could hear it rushing past and knew the current was moving dangerously fast. But neither did she want to be trapped inside the house. If the rescue personnel or Holt did succeed in reaching the house, they might not realize she was inside.

She had to get to the roof.

Inside, the water had almost reached the top of her boots and it was even higher on the other side of the door. She didn't think it was safe to open it. Holding the flashlight, she slogged her way through the kitchen to the bathroom at the rear of the house. Here, the window was set higher than the other windows and the water level hadn't yet reached the sill. Opening the sash, Jessie climbed out until she stood on the outer sill and clung to the roof gutter. The rain pummeled her as she got a toehold on the window frame and managed to pull herself up onto the low roof, scraping her hands and legs in the process. She crawled on her hands and knees to the highest point and grabbed hold of a vent stack that protruded through the roof. Then she hung on for dear life.

Jessie had no idea how long she clung to the vent pipe. Although the night air wasn't cold, the rain and fear chilled her until her teeth chattered. Her hands were slippery and she had a hard time holding on to the pipe. The darkness was deceptive, distorting her depth perception so that she could no longer tell how high the water was or how fast it was moving. But she could hear it, gurgling and splashing and rushing past the house. How far inland did the flood extend? Her cottage was situated on a low-lying stretch of land, but the main road was on higher ground. Surely, a rescue vehicle would be able to get close.

Suddenly, a light penetrated the gloom, illuminating the sheeting rain and swirling water. Jessie blinked rapidly, and then released the pipe with one hand long enough to wave frantically.

"Here!" she yelled, although she knew whoever it was couldn't possibly hear her. "I'm here!"

The light came closer and Jessie realized it was a small boat with two men in it. They wore yellow, reflective raincoats and the man in the front held up a massive spotlight. The boat pushed through the flood waters toward the house. For just an instant the spotlight swung away from her and Jessie could see who sat in the front of the boat.

Holt.

"Thank God," she whispered.

HOLT SWEPT THE spotlight over the house and, through the driving rain, he saw Jessie on the roof, clinging to a pipe. She raised a hand to let him know she was okay. Some of his anxiety subsided, but he wouldn't breathe easily again until he had her on solid ground and in his arms. The water had risen over the deck and reached the middle of the windows of the tiny cottage. As soon as he received Jessie's call, he and Evan had hitched the small boat they kept at the ranch to Evan's truck and raced to Jessie's house. The fire department had already arrived, but with the access road underwater, had been unable to reach the house. Two firefighters helped Holt and Evan launch the boat, while a third called in for air support, should they need it. Holt hoped to hell they wouldn't.

Now he assessed the situation. The current in the middle of the river was moving fast, but around the house it churned slightly less aggressively. Both he and Evan wore life jackets, and he'd brought an extra one for Jessie.

"I'll bring us right up to the side of the house," Evan shouted. "Can you reach the roof?"

As Evan motored the boat up alongside the cottage, Holt secured a length of rope and the spare life jacket over his shoulder and stood, taking care not to rock the boat any more than necessary. The rain was relentless, lashing at his face as he reached up and grabbed the edge of the roof.

"Don't move," he shouted to Jessie. "I'll come to you!"

Hoisting himself onto the roof, he made his way to where Jessie clung to the vent stack. Her bare legs were scraped and raw and her Western boots provided little traction on the rough shingles. As he reached her side, she released the pipe and flung her arms around his neck. They started to slide and Holt had to grab the pipe so that she didn't unbalance them both.

"You're here, you're really here!" Her voice caught on a suppressed sob.

"Of course I am, sweetheart," he reassured her, holding her tightly with one arm. "But you should know I charge a lot for roof rescues."

"Anything," she said. "Whatever you want!"

"Okay, I'll remind you that you said that later." Holt grinned. "But for now, we're going to get you down from here. Are you hurt?"

"N-no, just scared."

"Well, you don't need to be scared anymore. I'm here and in another few minutes you'll be in that boat and on your way to a nice, hot bath. Here, let me help you put this on." He placed the life jacket over her head and fastened it securely around her waist. Dropping the rope from his shoulder, he found the loose end. "I'm going to tie this around you," he said. "Just as a safety measure."

He passed the rope under her arms and created a secure loop. "Now, we're going to just take our time and inch our way toward the edge of the roof, okay? Then I'll lower you into the boat with Evan."

"Okay," she agreed.

Holding her against his chest, Holt used his body to shield her from the rough roof as they began inching their way toward the edge. Planting his heels against the lip of the gutter, he ran the loose end of the rope behind his back and looked at Evan. The rushing water would make it difficult to safely transfer Jessie onto the undulating boat. Even now, the small craft pitched back and forth in the current as Evan fought to keep it in one spot.

"Ready?"

"Hand her down!" Evan called. "I've got you, Jess!"

Holt helped Jessie scoot to the edge of the roof. "Turn onto your stomach. I'm going to lower you down."

Jessie did as he asked while he gripped her around her wrists. She locked her gaze on his. "I love you," she shouted, blinking at him through the rain. "I need you to know that, whatever happens."

Something tightened in his chest, like a coil that had been overwound. Then it snapped and broke free. When he spoke, his voice was rough with emotion. "I shouldn't have let you leave. I've been crazy about you for years." He began to lower her over the edge. "But I need you to get into that boat, Jessica."

"Holt—"

"Woman, would you please get in the damned boat?!"

The water level was high enough that, as Holt lowered her down, Evan managed to hook an arm around her hips. Holt released her, and both she and Evan fell backward, but managed to stay inside the small craft. Holt tossed the trailing end of rope down after her.

She was safe.

He barely had time to register the thought when he caught sight of a fallen tree at least sixty feet long, moving toward them in the current at an alarming rate. There wasn't enough time for him to climb into the boat, not the way it was pitching and rolling, and there was every chance the log would hit both the cottage and the boat.

"Evan," he shouted, pointing at the log. "Get her out of here!"

Evan spotted the tree moving swiftly in their direction. "Holt, jump!"

But it was too late. The massive roots of the log struck the corner of the house. Holt barely had time to brace himself for the impact when there was a loud cracking sound. The structure gave a shuddering heave and the entire house tilted at an alarming angle. Holt was thrown onto his back against the roof shingles as the pouring rain beat against his face. He rolled over and tried to regain his bearings, but the house shifted sideward, pitching him over the edge of the roof. He managed to grab on to the gutter as he fell, but realized the house had broken free from the pilings and now it spun in a slow arc. Below, he could hear the sloshing and gurgling of the river as it swept past, but the rain and the darkness and the angle of the house prevented him from seeing if Evan and Jessie had escaped the impact.

The water sucked at his legs as the house started to move downstream and he scrambled for a foothold, when suddenly the gutter began to pull away from the wall. Holt made a desperate grab for the roof, but his hands were slick and the suction of the current on his lower body too strong. The gutter ripped completely away and Holt's roar of denial was cut short as he plummeted backward and the dark, churning floodwaters closed over his head.

Chapter Sixteen

J ESSIE WATCHED IN horror as the cottage shuddered beneath the force of the impact. Evan gunned the motor and turned the boat away, but not before she saw Holt fall backward onto the roof. The entire house seemed to groan in protest and then the river slowly, inexorably sucked the structure from its mooring.

"Evan!" she shouted. "We have to go back! He's getting swept away!"

"There's too much debris!" He pointed at the massive tree that had swung around after hitting the house. Evan only just managed to get out of its path as it pivoted and threatened to block their escape. Now it rode the current alongside the small house as it began to move downstream. "We can't get close enough to pick him up. It's too dangerous! Holt knows the risks. He'll be okay!"

Jessie stared at Evan in disbelief. "Evan Claiborne, if you don't turn this boat around, I swear I'll do it for you! We need to go after him!"

Evan was a volunteer firefighter and she trusted him with her life, but this wasn't her life. This was Holt's. Even now the cottage was drifting farther away and visibility grew worse. Soon the small house would be gone.

"Please, Evan!"

She saw the indecision on his face as he aimed the spotlight downriver, but the rain made it nearly impossible to see anything.

"Okay!" he shouted, and handed the spotlight to her. "Keep the beam in front of us and hold on tight!"

He motored the small craft after the cottage, dodging debris in the water. As they drew closer to the drifting house, Jessie shone the spotlight over the roof but there was no sign of Holt.

"He must be in the water!" She trained the light onto the surface of the river. She saw tree limbs and logs and lawn furniture, but there was no sign of Holt.

"Please, please," Jessie chanted in a small, fervent prayer.

"There are first responders positioned downstream," Evan shouted to her. "If Holt makes it that far, they'll grab him!"

Jessie stared at him in disbelief. "What do you mean *if he makes it that far?*"

Through the sluicing rain, Evan's expression was somber. "I'm not going to lie to you, Jess. This is a dangerous situation. But if anyone can survive, Holt can. He grew up on this river. He's smart and he's strong."

"We have to keep going! At least until we reach the first responders. Please, Evan?"

After a second, Evan nodded. Lifting his handheld radio, he relayed the information to the firefighters on the road, and then grimly steered the little boat through the churning water, keeping an eye on any debris that might be coming up behind them. Several times they had to duck to avoid low-hanging tree limbs. But there was no sign of Holt. In the distance, Jessie could see the flashing red, blue, and yellow lights of the emergency vehicles positioned on the road, as close to the water as they could get.

Then her light picked up something reflective in the water, just a little ahead of the boat.

"There he is!" she cried, grabbing Evan's arm and pointing.

Evan maneuvered the craft next to Holt, who floated faceup in the water, unmoving.

"Help me get him into the boat!" Evan shouted.

Jessie heard the panic in his voice as they grabbed Holt by his life jacket and then Evan single-handedly dragged him on board, where he lay motionless on the floor. Jessie bent over him, noting the gray pallor of his skin.

"Hurry, Evan!"

As he gunned the motor toward the emergency vehicles, Jessie tried to remember what she knew about CPR. With the pelting rain and sloshing movement of the boat, she couldn't tell if Holt was breathing or not. There was a nasty gash on his head that disappeared beneath his hairline, and the water was tinged red where it trickled from his hair.

"Holt," she said urgently. "Holt, can you hear me?"

There was no response, and Jessie put her hand to his face, scared by how chilled his skin felt beneath her palm. Her own heart was racing with fear and adrenaline. Tipping Holt's head back, she pinched his nose shut, sealed her mouth over his, and blew air into his lungs. Her head felt light and it was as if she watched herself from somewhere outside of her own body, trying desperately to breathe life back into the man she loved.

The prow of the boat bumped against solid land. As Evan leaped out, two firefighters surged forward, lifted Holt out of the boat and carried him to a nearby stretcher, where emergency medical technicians quickly began working on him. But when Jessie would have scrambled after him, Evan held her back.

"Let them do their job, Jess."

Jessie allowed him to lead her up to the main road, where a firetruck and an ambulance waited. An EMT approached her and wrapped a thermal blanket around her shoulders.

"Those are some pretty nasty scrapes you have." The woman eyed Jessie's bare legs. "Come over here and let me take a better look."

Jessie reluctantly went with her, but couldn't tear her gaze from where Holt lay on the stretcher. She couldn't see him, surrounded as he was by medical personnel and firefighters.

As the EMT examined her scrapes, Jessie covered her mouth with her hands, more terrified than she had ever been in her entire life. Holt was so big and strong and solid, it seemed impossible that anything could hurt him. He'd saved her life. How was it possible that he was now fighting for his own? She didn't realize she'd begun to cry until someone pulled her into his arms. It was Luke.

"Hey, hey," he said, awkwardly patting her shoulder. "I

got here as quick as I could. If anyone can get through this, Holt can."

Jessie nodded mutely against his shoulder, but couldn't prevent her soft sobs. They watched as the EMTs worked over him for several more minutes. Then a path cleared as they lifted him into the ambulance. Pulling free from Luke, Jessie ran toward him. An oxygen mask covered Holt's nose and mouth, and a white bandage on his forehead stood out starkly against his dark hair, but as the EMTs settled him into the back of the vehicle, his eyes opened briefly.

He was alive.

"I'm riding with him," she insisted.

She clambered in beside him as an EMT closed the doors. The driver flipped on the siren and they began to move. Despite his tan, Holt's face looked bleached of color as he lay on the stretcher with his eyes closed. Blood seeped through the bandage on his forehead. The EMT took a seat on his other side and, after covering him with a thermal blanket, administered an IV drip. Jessie took Holt's hand in her own. He was so cold. She closed her fingers around his, willing her own warmth and life force into him.

"Holt," she said softly. "I'm here, baby."

His eyelids flickered. Then they opened and she found herself trapped in the dazzling blue depths of his eyes. Withdrawing his hand from her grasp, he reached up and pulled the oxygen mask away from his face. His movements were slow and deliberate, as if the action took all his strength.

"No, don't do that," Jessie chided. "You need to keep

that on."

"Can't," he croaked.

Jessie bent over him and taking care to avoid the bandage, smoothed his wet hair back from his face. "You're safe now. Don't talk, just rest."

He lifted his hand and stroked a finger over her damp cheek. "Don't cry."

A new rush of tears threatened as Jessie caught his hand in hers. She smiled at him through blurred vision. "They're happy tears, I promise. You're here and you're alive and that's all I care about."

"I have to tell you—" He broke off as a coughing spasm racked his large frame.

"Keep this on, please," the EMT said, replacing the oxygen mask. "We'll be at the hospital soon."

"Save your strength," Jessie urged. "I'm not going to leave you, Holt. I'll be right here."

Within minutes they were pulling up to the hospital and the doors of the ambulance opened. Jessie tried to stay with Holt as he was rushed into the emergency room, but found herself whisked aside by an ER nurse.

"I understand you were caught in the floodwater." The nurse's expression was sympathetic. "Let's find you some dry clothes and then we'll take a look at those scrapes."

"I'm fine. I need to go with him," Jessie protested, turning to watch as Holt's gurney was pushed down the corridor away from her. "I promised I wouldn't leave him."

"They'll be running some tests and you would only be in the way." The nurse rummaged through a cabinet and handed Jessie a set of blue scrubs. "Here you go. And here's a pair of hospital socks and a towel. I'll give you a few minutes to change. You can put your wet clothes in this plastic bag."

Alone in the small, curtained area, Jessie stripped out of her sodden clothes. Only then did she realize her legs were raw and abraded from the roof shingles. She pulled on the scrubs and was pushing her clothes into the plastic bag when the nurse reentered with a small tray of medical supplies.

"Just hop up here and I'll clean those scrapes."

Jessie did as she asked, wincing as the nurse pulled bits of asphalt and dirt out of the cuts before applying an antiseptic ointment and covering them with a light gauze pad.

"When can I see Holt?"

Before the nurse could reply, they heard a commotion in the hallway outside the exam area and then the curtains were pushed aside. Jessie's eyes widened as Luke, Evan, her parents and Rosa-Maria crowded forward.

"Jessie!" Gina cried and rushed to pull Jessie into an embrace. "Evan called us and we came right away. Are you hurt?"

"No, I'm fine," Jessie assured her. "Holt saved my life. He and Evan rescued me with a boat, but Holt was trapped on the roof when the cottage got swept away. Is he going to be okay?"

"The good news is that he has no water in his lungs, but they'll likely keep him overnight as a precaution," Luke said. "He has a mild concussion from the head injury."

"When can I see him?"

"They're stitching his head now. Dad is with him."

Jessie's father came forward and kissed her forehead. "You're a brave young woman, Jessie, to have climbed onto the roof and stayed there as long as you did."

Jessie shook her head. "That wasn't bravery, that was necessity. The river rose so fast, I didn't have time to leave. Evan and Holt are the brave ones. They risked their lives to save me. If anything had happened to Holt—"

She broke off, unable to continue. Unable to even go down that dark path.

"I told you he'd be okay," Luke said. "Good thing he's so hardheaded."

They turned as Dr. Wallace approached and shook hands with Luke and Evan. "Seems like I just saw all of you here not that long ago," he said with a smile. "You can see Holt now. His lungs are clear and, aside from the mild concussion and some minor bumps and bruises, he's okay. I expect him to make a full recovery."

"Thank the Lord," Rosa-Maria said fervently.

Dr. Wallace glanced between Jessie and the others. "I'd tell you to keep your visit short, but somehow I don't think that's going to happen."

"SON, I KNOW you don't want to be here but you'll be home a lot sooner if you just follow the doctor's orders and get some rest." Gus eased himself into the chair next to Holt's bed. "You've taken a pretty good blow to the head and you were found unconscious in the water. No medical professional is going to release you tonight, nor should you want them to. Not after what you've been through."

Holt felt like he'd been hit with a wrecking ball, but he wouldn't admit that to his father. After falling into the river, he'd managed to resurface and had fought to reach the shore even as the current swept him downstream. He'd spotted the search lights of the rescue personnel but, as he'd struggled to reach them, something had struck him hard. The next thing he remembered was waking up on the ground with the emergency personnel bent over him. He'd been amazed to hear that Jessie had been the one to spot him and that she and Evan had pulled him from the water. He knew he was lucky to be alive.

"I feel fine."

A brief smile curved his Gus's mouth. "Sure you do. And you'll feel even better after a good night's rest."

"There's no such thing as a good night's rest in the hospital," Holt grumbled. "I need to see Jessica."

"She's getting checked out by one of the ER nurses." Gus raised his hands at Holt's look of alarm. "Nothing serious, just a few scrapes. She's going to be fine, thanks to you."

"If it wasn't for me, she never would have left Riverrun," Holt said morosely. "I was a jackass."

"You're only human, son." Gus removed his Western hat and placed it on a nearby table before he crossed one leg over the other and considered Holt thoughtfully. "You've been hurt and there's no shame in trying to protect your heart. What do think I've been doing for the past twenty-plus years?"

Holt's interest was piqued in spite of himself. His father rarely, if ever, talked about himself or his failed relationships. "Is there something you want to tell me? Maybe about what's really going on between you and Rosa-Maria?"

To his astonishment, his father's cheeks turned ruddy, but his smile broadened. "Ah, yes. I suspected Jessie saw us together in Rosa-Maria's hospital room."

"So she was right when she said you two had a thing for each other?"

"I've loved Rosa-Maria for longer than I can remember," Gus acknowledged. "I tried to deny it, to fight it, even told myself a hundred different reasons why it would never work out. That's why she left, because she'd finally had enough of my foolishness."

"So what's changed?"

Gus shifted. "I had an epiphany the day she had a heart attack. An awakening. Neither one of is getting any younger and I might have lost her without ever having told her how I felt." He gave a rueful laugh. "But I still didn't get it, not entirely. I admitted that I love her, but I also told her I didn't think I could risk getting married again. That's when she chose not to return to the ranch, and I've regretted it every minute since."

"So . . .?"

"So I asked her to marry me."

Holt couldn't prevent his grin. "Congratulations. I'm really happy for you. For both of you. We all love Rosa-Maria. Have you told the others?"

"Oh, yes, everyone knows except you and Jessie, although she's probably heard the happy news by now." He paused. "So what about you, son?"

Holt shifted uncomfortably. "What do you mean?"

"I've had a wake-up call. I don't intend to spend one more day without the woman I love, and neither should you."

Holt drew in a deep breath and blew it out slowly. There was no question he'd had his own wake-up call. He could so easily have lost Jessica. But before he could reply, the door opened and suddenly she was there. Holt was vaguely aware that his brothers, Rosa-Maria, and Jessie's parents were also filing into the small room, but he only had eyes for Jessica, looking both disheveled and adorable in a pair of oversized hospital scrubs.

Her eyes locked on to his and her face crumpled as she launched herself across the small space and into his arms.

"Holt." Her voice was muffled against his chest. "Don't you ever, ever do that to me again!"

Nothing had ever felt as good as Jessie did in his arms. She was safe and she was *here*. She raised her face and the expression in her dark eyes made his heart clench hard in his chest.

"Holt—"

"Shh. There's something I need to say." Pulling back just a bit, he surveyed her. Over her head, he watched his father and brothers and Jessie's family slowly retreat from the room and quietly close the door behind them. He tucked a tangled strand of Jessie's still-damp hair behind her ear and swallowed hard. "I love you, Jessica Montero. I think I have for a long time. I've been an idiot and I realized it the morning you left the ranch."

"Do you want to know why I left? After that night, I knew we were going to be seeing more of each other." She gave him a meaningful look. "A lot more. But I didn't want to disrespect your father while I was technically working for him and living under his roof. I wanted a relationship with you that had nothing to do with my working at the ranch."

"You wanted me to woo you," Holt said, smiling.

"Yes."

Holt pulled her closer as he struggled to put unfamiliar feelings into words. "I've spent so many years keeping people—*women*—away, that it's become second nature. I don't want to have my heart broken, but I'm afraid that's what will happen if you make me live without you. I love you, Jessica, and I need you in my life."

"You've got me," she assured him. "You had me at *tequila*."

Holt laughed, bemused and relieved. "What?"

"That night at the cantina, when you ordered a tequila and I brought you a top-shelf brand."

Holt laughed softly, remembering his surprise when he'd sipped the expensive liquor, knowing what she'd done. "I deserved that." Tipping her face up, he searched her eyes. "I hope I can deserve you."

"You can start by kissing me."

Holt did, very thoroughly.

Epilogue

THREE MONTHS HAD passed since the river had swept Jessie's rental cottage away. The floodwaters had receded in a few days and the landlord was already in the process of rebuilding the house, stronger and better, and a little farther back from the river than before. Now, on this beautiful, sunny October day, Jessie had difficulty believing there had ever been a time when the skies had been gray and stormy. Three dozen white chairs had been set up on the sweeping lawn of Riverrun Ranch. Beneath a flower-bedecked trellis, with the now-calm waters of the Pedernales sparkling in the background, Gus and Rosa-Maria exchanged wedding vows in front of their families and closest friends.

Jessie stood to one side, holding her grandmother's bridal bouquet, but her eyes were on the best man. Holt looked handsome in a black jacket and crisp white shirt and she privately thought the new scar on his forehead gave him a rakish, slightly piratical look. As if he sensed her watching him, Holt lifted his gaze to hers. His blue eyes grew heated before he dropped one eyelid in an audacious wink.

As the minister pronounced them husband and wife, Gus swept Rosa-Maria into his arms for a gusty kiss and the guests burst into spontaneous applause. Jessie sprang forward to give her grandmother the bouquet of flowers and then she and Holt fell into step behind them as they made their way to the ranch house, where a brunch buffet would be served on the terrace.

Holt captured her hand in his own and bent his head to speak softly in her ear. "You look beautiful, sweetheart. That dress looks real pretty on you."

Jessie swept a hand over the pale-pink organza gown that left her shoulders bare. "Thank you. You clean up pretty well yourself, cowboy."

As the wedding guests followed the bride and groom to the house, Holt drew Jessie aside, tugging her along a path that led to the water's edge.

"Where are we going?" she asked, laughing. "We'll miss the opening toasts."

"They can't start without me. I'm the best man."

"You'll get no argument from me there," Jessie said, smiling. "I've known that for a long time. But I still need to oversee the buffet preparations!"

Rosa-Maria had asked Jessie to prepare the wedding menu, featuring the same food she served from her shiny new food truck. Jessie had purchased the truck several weeks after the flood and had sent it out for a custom-wrap that featured bold, Mexican colors and the name Jessie's Cocina emblazoned across the side. She'd been in business for almost two months and she'd never been happier. The food truck had been an instant hit and business had been brisk wherever she went. She'd spent the previous day stocking the ranch kitchen with food for the buffet, and her father had enlisted the kitchen staff from Rosa's Cantina to do the actual cooking.

"You have some of the best cooks I know taking care of the buffet. Just enjoy yourself." Holt drew her to a stop on the edge of the lawn and turned her to face him. "With your new business and all the wedding preparations, it seems like ages since I've had you to myself."

In fact, it had been just two days. After the flood, Jessie had moved back home with her parents until she could find another place to live, but she and Holt managed to make time to be together every day. He had spent the past three months wooing her with a sweetness that stole her heart. There had been picnics and moonlit drives, and so many kisses. The past two days had been the exception, due to the wedding preparations.

"It sounds as if you might miss me," Jessie said, looking at him from beneath her lashes. She wrapped her arms around his waist and tipped her face up to his. "Don't worry; once I find a place to live, we can be together every night."

Holt's father wasn't old-fashioned and likely wouldn't know or care if Jessie chose to spend the night at Riverrun Ranch, but Jessie's family was another issue altogether. Out of respect for her more-conservative father and grandmother, she made sure she was home each night, but the strain was telling, and she knew Holt's patience was beginning to wear thin.

"What if I told you I've found a place for you?" Holt asked.

Jessie leaned back in his arms. "Will I like it?"

Holt smiled and nuzzled the sensitive skin of her neck. "I think so."

"When can I see it?"

In answer, Holt turned her around and pointed in the direction of the foreman's cabin. "The cabin's been empty since Luke and Jorie moved out. I thought it might be perfect for us."

"Us?"

Jessie didn't want to tell Holt that no matter how much her father liked him, he wouldn't approve of them living together. She was a grown woman, but she didn't want to go against her family's traditional values, no matter how tempting the offer.

"I was going to wait," Holt said, "but seeing how happy my father is made me realize that I don't want to put this off any longer."

Jessie turned as Holt withdrew a small velvet box from his jacket. Her heart skipped a beat and then began pounding in her chest like a herd of stampeding cattle.

"Holt—"

"I love you. I have for a long time." He went down on one knee on the grassy knoll and opened the box to reveal a single, stunning solitaire that sparkled in the sunshine. He held it out to her and Jessie had never seen his expression so earnest or so serious. "Marry me, Jessica. The sooner, the better, because I don't think I can wait much longer."

Jessie covered her mouth with her both hands as she stared, speechless, at the man who knelt before her. "Oh,

Holt . . ."

"Just say yes, darlin'."

His easy words belied the anxiety she saw in his blue eyes. Heedless of her bridesmaid gown, Jessie fell to her knees and threw her arms around his neck.

"Yes, a thousand times, *yes*!"

He exhaled in relief and then he was kissing her more sweetly than he'd ever kissed her before.

"Here, let's get this on your finger before you come to your senses and change your mind," he muttered. He slid the ring on with hands that trembled. Jessie held her hand up to admire the stone and how it caught the light.

"Oh, it's beautiful," she breathed. "I love you, Holt Claiborne."

Holt grinned and helped her to her feet, wrapping her in his arms. "Well, for better or worse, you've got me."

"I think you mean I've *caught* you." Jessie smiled up at him. "You're the best thing that's ever been fished out of that old river. I think I'll keep you."

Holt laughed and together they walked hand in hand toward the ranch and a new life together.

The End

Want more? Check out Luke and Jorie's story in
Counting on the Cowboy!

Join Tule Publishing's newsletter for more great reads and
weekly deals!

If you enjoyed *How to Catch a Cowboy,*
you'll love the other books in....

The Riverrun Ranch series

Book 1: *Swipe Right for a Cowboy*

Book 2: *Counting on the Cowboy*

Book 3: *How to Catch a Cowboy*

Available now at your favorite online retailer!

More books by Karen Foley

The Glacier Creek series

Book 1: *Montana Defender*

Book 2: *Montana Firefighter*

Book 3: *Montana Protector*

Available now at your favorite online retailer!

About the Author

Karen Foley admits to being an incurable romantic. When she's not working for the Department of Defense, she loves writing sexy stories about alpha heroes and strong heroines. Karen lives in New England with her husband, two daughters, and a houseful of pets.

Thank you for reading

How to Catch a Cowboy

If you enjoyed this book, you can find more from all our great authors at TulePublishing.com, or from your favorite online retailer.

TULE
PUBLISHING

Made in the USA
Monee, IL
28 July 2021